BBC

DOCTOR WHO

Plague of the Cybermen

Also available from Broadway:

The Dalek Generation *by Nicholas Briggs*

Shroud of Sorrow *by Tommy Donbavand*

BBC

DOCTOR WHO

Plague of the Cybermen

JUSTIN RICHARDS

Broadway Paperbacks
New York

Copyright © 2013 by Justin Richards

All right reserved.
Published in the United States by Broadway Paperbacks,
an imprint of the Crown Publishing Group,
a division of Random House, Inc., New York.
www.crownpublishing.com

Broadway Paperbacks and its logo, a letter B bisected on the diagonal,
are trademarks of Random House, Inc.

This edition published by arrangement with BBC Books, an imprint of
Ebury Publishing, a division of the Random House Group Limited, London.

Doctor Who is a BBC Wales production for BBC One.
Executive producers: Steven Moffat and Caroline Skinner.

BBC, DOCTOR WHO, and TARDIS (word marks, logos, and devices) are
trademarks of the British Broadcasting Corporation and are used under license.
Cybermen originally created by Kit Pedler and Gerry Davis.

Library of Congress Cataloging-in-Publication Data is available upon request.

ISBN 978-0-385-34676-4
eISBN 978-0-385-34677-1

Printed in the United States of America

Editorial director: Albert DePetrillo
Series consultant: Justin Richards
Project editor: Steve Tribe
Cover design: Lee Binding © Woodlands Books Ltd. 2013
Production: Alex Goddard

1   3   5   7   9   10   8   6   4   2

First Edition

For the Doctor
A friend and mentor throughout the last fifty years

Prologue

In a landscape bled of all colour, Stefan was digging his own grave. The swirling fog muffled the sound of the spade as it bit into the cold ground. The pile of earth beside the grave rose higher as the grave got deeper.

Gravestones stood as silent sentries, dark grey against the lighter shade of the air. Pitted, cracked and broken. Beyond them, the vague pencil-drawn shape of the remains of the church. A hint of the jagged, fractured tower. A suggestion of the empty, sightless windows and crumbling walls.

Stefan paid it no heed. His whole world was focused into the dark pit he was digging.

'Dig it deep,' Old Nicolai had said. 'Dig it deep so the plague stays buried with her. We've lost enough good people already.'

The plague was keeping Stefan busy but, he had to admit, you could have too much of a bad thing. Yesterday young Liza, tomorrow – who could guess? Probably Magda, who was already sick, already as grey as the fog swirling over the grave.

Stefan kept digging, until he needed his short wooden ladder to climb out of the pit and rest a moment. His forehead was moist, sweat mingling with the condensing fog. If it wasn't fog it would be a storm. The fog was damp and clammy and seemed to drain the life from their surroundings. But Stefan preferred the fog to the angry thunder, the stabbing lightning, the rain so heavy it stung his arms and face as he worked and filled up the hole as quickly as he dug it.

Just a few more inches, he decided. Just to be on the safe side. It was a decision that killed him.

He clambered back down into the pit. The air was thinning, and the first spots of rain splashed onto the hard-packed soil. Finish this quick, Stefan thought. Finish this quick and get to the tavern before Gustav shuts up for the night. He could already taste the warm, bitter ale. Could already smell the lamb broth.

A few last shovelfuls of earth. Stefan slammed his spade down into the heavy clay.

Clang!

The impact jarred right up his arm, tingling in his shoulder and jolting his wrist. It sounded like he'd hit metal. Maybe it was another Talisman. He prayed he'd not damaged it. He had no use for such trinkets but enough people did that he could get a good price for a Talisman. Exploring with the shovel, he gently tapped at the bottom of the grave. Earth here, then something solid.

Stefan leaned the shovel against the side of the grave and knelt down. There was just room for him to scrabble at the ground with his hands. Just enough light, as the fog cleared and the moon broke through, for him to see the glint of metal. The rain was getting heavier, washing the fog from the air and the earth from the metal surface as Stefan uncovered it.

Gently, carefully, he smoothed away the dirt from a long sliver of metal. Beside it, another one. And another. They were connected at one end, he realised as he scraped. Jointed along their length. Rain ran down his face, blurring his vision, matting his hair. He wiped it away, the rough dirt scraping at his skin. He'd look a mess when he got to the tavern.

Now the whole shape was visible. Silver fingers. The back of a hand – a gauntlet? Part of a suit of armour perhaps...

Stefan straightened up, easing his back. He shook the rain from his hair, wiped his forehead on his sleeve, and knelt again to examine his find. Rain was pooling in the upturned palm of the gauntlet, distorting the tracery of lines and joints. The design was intricate but robust. A work of art, but somehow brutal and powerful too.

Stefan frowned… But – hadn't the glove been palm *down* when he uncovered it? He leaned forward, looking closer, blinking the rain away.

The fingers flexed. A sudden, spasmodic movement. Stefan gasped and jerked backwards. But the fingers were still again.

Was it his imagination? Or had his weight on the surrounding soil moved it? Again, he leaned closer, the rain beating down on the back of his head and running down his neck like a cold chill of terror along his spine. The hand *shivered*. The slightest movement, but movement nevertheless. This time, Stefan did not pull away.

And the hand thrust suddenly upwards, out of the ground, clamping round his throat.

He tried to cry out, but couldn't draw the breath he needed. Couldn't breathe at all. His hands scrabbled desperately as he was dragged down. The earth around the metal gauntlet crumbled away. Hand and arm were uncovered. A torso. The armoured silver head punching up through the ground, right in front of Stefan's terrified face.

Empty eyes. Gaping mouth. A metal skull.

His hand closed on the handle of the shovel. Somehow he managed to lift it. Somehow he managed to swing it one-handed at the metal creature that held him tight. The shovel blade connected with the arm. The sound of the impact was muffled. Stefan's vision was blurred. Rain in his eyes, and the last vestiges of the fog creeping in as he gasped and choked.

Then he was being dragged down into the earth. Feeling the coarse soil graze his face. Glimpses of silver as the life ebbed away.

Fog.

Darkness.

Death…

Chapter 1

The stranger just *was*. No one saw him arrive. No one remembered him shouldering his way to the counter or asking Gustav for a drink. No one really noticed him at all as he sat at a table in the corner of the bar.

Which was odd, because Klimtenburg was exactly the sort of small community where a stranger could expect to be noticed. Everyone knew everyone. The single unnamed tavern should have fallen silent the moment an outsider stepped across the threshold.

Yet, the recognition was gradual. There was no 'We don't have strangers here' moment. No sudden, awkward silence. No simultaneous turn of every head to see who had arrived unbidden and unwanted. It was as if the plague itself had taken on human form and solidified into being at the corner table of Gustav's tavern. Unnoticed until it was too late to root it out.

But slowly, people did notice. Old Nicolai hesitated, tankard halfway to his mouth as he frowned. Several others turned to look. Even Gustav himself paused as he poured a drink and tried to work out if the man looked familiar or if he just had that sort of face.

The stranger himself gradually seemed to notice the interest in him, the slow decrease in background volume as people stopped talking.

'It's the bow tie, isn't it?' he said when almost everyone was staring. 'I bet it's the bow tie. You're all looking at my bow tie, thinking, "What a cool fashion accessory, I just wish we had bow ties here in…"' He paused to take a careful sip of his drink. 'Er, where are we, actually?'

'You're in my tavern,' Gustav said, voice grating with suspicion.

'Really?' He seemed genuinely surprised. 'A tavern. With drinks and everything. No dominoes or darts, though. But don't worry, they'll come. And big-screen sports entertainment too – all sorts of things to save you having to actually talk to each other. Or admire other people's bow ties.'

Everyone continued to stare.

'Well, if it's your tavern,' the stranger went on, 'then it's you I have to thank for this quite excellent drink.' He took another swig. 'Yes, definitely. I can tell from the quality. This must be vintage.'

'Vintage?' Gustav's brow furrowed. 'What are you drinking?'

'Well, it's water actually. But quality will out.'

'Who are you?' Old Nicolai growled.

The stranger grinned, pointing both index fingers at Nicolai. 'Ooh, introductions. Great idea. We all know Gustav, because he's *Mein Host*, so I'll go next.' He straightened his bow tie and stuck out his impressive chin. 'I'm the Doctor. But you can all call me "the Doctor"… Next.'

'The Doctor?' Jan swayed slightly as he tried to take this in.

'The Doctor…' other people whispered to each other.

'Um…' the Doctor said as he watched his name ripple through the tavern. 'Problem?'

'Doctor,' Old Nicolai said, walking across to take the seat next to the stranger. 'Thank God you're here.'

She was used to the sounds of drunken men staggering home from the tavern. Sometimes they held loud conversations that made no sense. Sometimes they fell over. Sometimes they sang. But they never, ever hammered on Olga's front door and shouted that she was needed in the tavern right away.

Except tonight.

Olga pulled her long coat on over her nightgown and stuffed her bare feet into her boots. It was hard enough getting up in the morning, let alone the middle of the night. And this was the first night in a week that there wasn't actually a storm. Though even as she thought it, there was a distant rumble of thunder from somewhere over the mountains.

She was pleased to see it was Klaus. There had been a time, many years ago… But they had grown old together and Olga knew they had both missed the moment. He smiled when she opened the door, and for a brief moment in the half-light he was the boy she'd laughed and joked and played with. Then he turned to nod towards the tavern, and the years piled back on, turning him middle-aged in an instant.

'What is it?' she asked. 'It's a long time since you visited me in the middle of the night.'

She thought he might smile at that. But his face remained stern and solemn. 'You'd best come,' he said. 'The Doctor's here.'

Olga closed her eyes and let the relief wash over her. 'The Doctor. We'll be all right now, then.'

'Old Nicolai said you should come because you knew Vadim better than any of us.'

Old Nicolai, Klaus and Olga the schoolteacher stood watching as the Doctor examined Stefan's body.

'We sent for medical help months ago,' Klaus said. 'When it was clear the plague was back.'

'What took you so long?' Old Nicolai wanted to know.

The Doctor tapped his chin with a chunky metal wand he took from his pocket. 'Message didn't get to me. I don't usually do *medical*.'

'But you are a physician? You said you were a doctor.'

'Oh yes, I'm a doctor. *The* Doctor. Physician? Well, more of a physician than anyone else you've got here, I'd guess.'

'Vadim was one of the first to die,' Klaus said. 'A long time ago now. But Olga here knew him best.'

'He was a doctor?'

'Claimed to be,' Olga said. 'Not sure what qualifications he actually had, but he knew how to mix potions and bathe wounds. He could keep leeches and…'

'OK, OK,' the Doctor cut her off. 'Think I've heard enough for a diagnosis. Leeches are *so* last year. But I would like to know what happened—'

'I told you,' Klaus cut in. 'He died of the plague. Vadim was one of the first.'

'Would like to know,' the Doctor went on, ignoring the interruption, 'what happened to this church.'

'The church?'

They all looked round at the cracked and

17

crumbling walls. The body was laid out in the crypt, one of the few intact areas of the building. Flickering candles gave the whole underground chamber an eerie and unsettling feel. Above them, the nave roof was gone, along with most of the windows and parts of the walls. The top of the tower looked like it had been bitten off by some ancient giant, and the remains of the structure leaned at a worrying angle.

'Story is, it was struck by a mighty force of fire from the sky,' Klaus explained.

'A storm,' Old Nicolai said. A rumble of thunder punctuated his words. 'We get more storms here than anywhere I know of.'

'You travelled then?'

'When I was younger,' the old man replied.

'Me too,' the Doctor said. 'And when I was older as well.'

'Are you suggesting the plague is a judgement on us?' Olga asked. 'The wrath of God visited on us for not repairing the church?'

'We can't rule anything out,' the Doctor told her. 'Nothing at all, nothing whatsoever. But no.'

'So what *can* you tell us?' Klaus asked.

'I can tell you one thing. This man didn't die of the plague. And I suspect you know that.'

No one spoke.

The Doctor walked slowly round the stone table where the body lay. 'I mean, you'll have noticed that his chest is ripped open and various organs torn out. And you don't need the *Observer Book of Dead Bodies* to tell you that one of his legs is missing. I'm assuming from the wound that he had a full set when he was alive.'

They all nodded.

'Less obvious, perhaps, is that it was removed by an expert. Quite a tidy job actually. I mean – considering they cut off his whole *leg*.'

'Plague Warriors,' Klaus said. He closed his eyes and crossed himself quickly.

'Plague Warriors – what's those?'

'That's what we call them,' Old Nicolai said. 'No one's seen them properly.'

'Another legend,' Olga said. 'No one's seen them *at all*. It's a way of explaining how the plague travels, how accidents happen. Scary stories to keep the children in order.'

'Don't need stories for that,' Klaus said quietly. 'Their teacher is scary enough.'

Old Nicolai went to stand beside the Doctor. 'So how did he die? Was it the loss of his leg? The wounds to his chest?'

'Good question.'

'You got a good answer?'

'Don't know if it's *good*. But he was strangled. See the bruising round the throat. Windpipe's pretty much crushed.'

'That take a lot of strength?' Klaus wondered.

'Oh yes.'

'A man, then.' Olga's tone suggested she'd never doubted it.

'Not necessarily,' the Doctor murmured.

The Doctor was keen to meet anyone who was suffering from the plague. Whether he could help them, Olga didn't know. But Magda and her husband Ivan lived close to the church. Dawn was breaking, but dark clouds hung heavy in the sky.

'I suspect there's a storm coming,' the Doctor said.

'There's always a storm coming,' Old Nicolai told him.

'Well, there are storms and then there are storms. I can't believe you took me to see a dead body before trying to help the living,' he went on. He sounded surprised rather than angry. 'The dead can always wait.'

'True,' Klaus said. 'But they do start to stink. And we want him in the ground before another nightfall.'

'What happens at nightfall?' the Doctor asked.

'The walking dead,' Olga said with a snort of annoyance. 'Another myth.'

'I'm sure you're right,' Klaus agreed. 'But I'd rather not take any chances.'

'Well, with only one leg he'll be the hopping dead at best,' the Doctor said. 'He was the gravedigger, right? So – who's going to dig *his* grave?'

Nicolai chuckled. 'You're practical, I'll give you

that.' He slapped Klaus on the shoulder. 'I'll give you a hand, Klaus.'

'Like you can dig, old man,' Klaus told him.

'I can keep you company. And I can tell you more stories. Come on – let's get started. No time like the present. The Doctor and Olga can tend to Magda well enough without us.'

The Doctor and Olga walked on in silence, until the Doctor asked: 'Where was he found?'

'Stefan? In the churchyard. He'd just dug poor Liza's grave. She died of the plague a few days ago.'

'Can I see her body?'

'Only if you can persuade Klaus to dig it up again for you.'

'The church – is there a priest to go with it?'

Olga shook her head. 'Not any more. Not for years and years. We all make peace with God in our own way. At Easter and Christmas most of us make the journey to Malkeburg. And if there's a burial… Well, Old Nicolai says a few words. Something appropriate.'

'He'd be good at that,' the Doctor said.

Ivan opened the door to them. He looked tired, and so pale his features were almost grey. Olga had already told the Doctor that the man seemed to be pining away in sympathy for his wife.

Magda was confined to bed. Too weak even to speak more than a few words. Her grey, emaciated hands lay on the folded-back sheets. She wore a high-collared nightgown, its white lace contrasting with her grey skin.

'The discoloration…?' the Doctor said quietly.

'It's the first sign.' Olga glanced at Magda's husband standing behind them, leaning against the doorframe for support. 'The skin gets darker as the disease spreads. They just get weaker and weaker then, until…'

The Doctor nodded slowly. He held one of Magda's hands, gently stroking it, murmuring quietly to her. The woman's face seemed to relax at his words. There was even the hint of a smile. Olga wondered what he had said.

In a few moments, Magda was sleeping peacefully. Ivan left them to it, shuffling out of the room. Once he was gone, the Doctor took his metal wand from his pocket. One end glowed as he swept it over the woman's body. He frowned.

'Sonic screwdriver,' he said, as if that explained it. 'Just need to change a few settings.'

This time, the wand clicked as he moved it. Just a few clicks at first, then, as the Doctor brought it closer to Magda, the clicking increased in speed and got louder. It was loudest and fastest over her chest. The Doctor put the wand away, and gently pulled back the covers.

'What is that?' he demanded.

Olga leaned over to see. 'It's her Talisman.'

The Doctor reached out for it, but drew back

before his fingers reached the Talisman. It hung round Magda's neck on a thin silver chain. The Talisman was circular, made of metal so bright it almost glowed. The surface was pitted and marked. In the centre was engraved a symbol, a circle with sections marked like the way you might cut a cake.

'Talisman? Where did she get it, do you know?'

'From Vadim.'

'I thought he was the physician.'

'Vadim's wife made them. He found the Talisman and his wife Nefta worked it into jewellery. In this case, a necklace.'

The Doctor's mouth dropped open. 'In *this* case? You mean there are others?'

'Oh yes. Vadim found many of these metal pieces.'

'Where?'

'Near the churchyard.'

'And his wife made them into jewellery.'

'She asked a fair price. She said they would bring good luck. Wealth and… love.'

The Doctor reached out and took Olga's hands. He pulled her gently closer to him. If anyone else had done that she'd have been embarrassed and annoyed. But it seemed natural and friendly.

'Do you have a Talisman?' he asked, and his voice was low and urgent.

'No. I don't… That is, I never…'

'You're not vain. Very wise.'

'It's not vanity. It's just, I have no one to impress.'

She blinked. She shouldn't have said that. Why did she say that?

'Oh, that's true,' the Doctor said, and his words felt like a punch.

Olga pulled her hands free of him.

'You don't need to impress them with Talismans. Talismen. Talismans... Whatever. You don't need to impress them because Klaus and Nicolai and the others are already in awe of you.'

He turned away, so he probably didn't see her surprise.

'You must be one hell of a teacher. The other plague victims,' he went on before she could comment on that, 'did they all have a Talisman?'

'I don't know.' She tried to think. 'Probably. I think so.'

'Vadim is dead, but his wife...' The Doctor sighed loudly and slapped his forehead with the palm of his hand. 'She's dead too, of course. Probably died before Vadim.'

'Yes, but how did you know?'

'Because this isn't plague, it's... How to explain?' The Doctor was pacing up and down. He paused beside the bed, reached down and took hold of the Talisman round Magda's neck. He looked at it for a moment, holding it carefully and gently. Then he yanked hard, breaking the chain.

'What are you doing?'

'You got a lead-lined box?' the Doctor demanded.

'What?'

'Or a toffee tin? No?' He rummaged through his pockets, finding a bag made of a strange yellow shiny material. He put the Talisman inside. 'It'll do for now. But I'd better get it back to… Actually,' he decided, 'we need to find every Talisman and get them all back to… Back to where I'm staying.'

'Where *are* you staying?' Olga wondered.

'Guest house.'

'We don't have a guest house.'

'That's all right. I brought my own. This isn't plague,' he added quietly. 'It's poison.'

'Can you cure it?'

'No. It's Hapthoid Radiation Sickness. This "Talisman" as you call it is the main locking bolt for the access panel of a Hapthoid reactor unit. There is no cure. But I can stop anyone else getting it.'

Olga looked at Magda. She seemed so peaceful, so calm. 'And what about Magda?'

The Doctor put his hand on her shoulder, following Olga's gaze. 'I'm sorry,' he said quietly. 'She died while we were talking.'

Chapter 2

The school was a single room – in fact, it was also Olga's living room. There were six children in the village, but Hans rarely came to school. The Doctor had liked Olga's suggestion that the children could help gather up the poisoned jewellery.

'Just so long as they don't touch it.' He had a stack of the shiny yellow bags to hand out. 'Proximity is only lethal over a prolonged period of time, but direct contact could be a problem. Best take no chances.'

Olga pointed out that one of the children already had her own Talisman. Jedka was wearing a bracelet of the shiny metal. She was reluctant to part with it until the Doctor crouched down at her level.

'It's all right,' he assured her. 'I speak 7-year-old like a native. And so I know you'll understand when I tell you how important it is that you put your bracelet in this bag.'

'You just want my bracelet.'

'No, I just want you not to get sick. You are one of the very most important people here in the village and you are in fact the very first person I want not to get sick – by being the very first and most important person to put their Talisman in a special bag.'

Jedka bit her lower lip and said nothing.

'Everyone is watching,' the Doctor went on. 'All your friends are here to see you start this off. You, Jedka, *you* are the person who will show the grown-ups what they need to do.'

'It's called setting an example,' Olga added.

'Like when Heini had to be good and set an example?'

'That's right. Except, I know *you* can do it.'

One of the boys shifted uncomfortably and muttered what might have been an apology.

Jedka nodded, and slipped off her bracelet. There was a grey mark where it had been. Olga looked at the Doctor – were they in time? He smiled and nodded and patted Jedka on the head.

It wasn't as easy with all the villagers. Some were unwilling to part with what they saw as precious and luck-bringing items of jewellery. But most, encouraged by Olga and Klaus, were happy to be rid of what could be causing them illness and pain, or might in the near future.

'The levels of irradiation vary a lot,' the Doctor said as the children set off round the village to gather pieces of jewellery. Olga didn't know what he meant. 'That's why the symptoms emerge over different timescales. Some of it is almost safe. But "almost" isn't good enough.'

Heini came to find them as they left Gustav collecting up jewellery from the people in the tavern at lunchtime.

'Lagis won't give Jedka her brooch.'

'She can be quite strong-willed,' Olga warned the Doctor. 'She suspects everyone is out for themselves.'

'Judges them according to her own standards, perhaps?'

Lagis stood in her yard, arms folded, a basket of washing waiting to be hung out – even though it was spotting with rain and the clouds still loomed menacingly.

In front of her, Jedka was holding out her yellow bag. She shook it. 'You have to give me the brooch. The Doctor says so.'

'And how do I know he doesn't just want it for himself?' Lagis demanded.

Olga had the feeling this exchange had been repeated several times already.

Jedka sighed. 'He just wants you not to get sick.'

'That's right,' the Doctor said. He grinned like it

was the biggest joke ever. 'But if you want to keep your brooch, well that's just fine.'

Lagis frowned and straightened her shoulders. 'Oh?'

'Yeah, no problem at all. Of course,' he added, 'you *will* get sick. Maybe not today or even this year. But one day. Very sick. And until you do, none of the other villagers will come near you. Not if you're wearing that brooch. And when you do get ill, none of them will come to help you then either. Not if you've still got the brooch. Unless it's to say "We told you so".' He nodded and grinned some more. 'So, you keep it if you want. We'll just get out of your way. *Right* out of your way. For good.'

The Doctor gently pulled Jedka back, and motioned for Olga to come with them.

'That grey patch of skin, under where you wear the brooch,' the Doctor said. 'You can see the same stain on Jedka's wrist when she holds out that yellow bag. It's where she wore a bracelet. But, hey – maybe Jedka knows what's good for her. Of course the stain on her skin will shrink and fade now the bracelet's gone. But yours will get bigger, you know. Bigger and darker...'

As they retreated, Lagis took a step towards them. Jedka gave a little gasp of fright. Then, face set, she held out the bag again.

Lagis tore off her brooch and dropped it in the bag.

'Thank you,' the Doctor said. 'You won't regret it.'

Lagis turned back to her washing. 'I never liked that brooch,' she said.

By mid afternoon, the Doctor reckoned he and his new friends had collected up all the jewellery they could find in the village.

'Are you going up to the castle?' Jedka asked.

'Is there a castle? I love castles. Castles are just so cool.'

'I've never been to the castle,' Jedka said. 'If you do go, can I come? I want to see the witch.'

Olga laughed. 'More stories,' she told the Doctor. 'There's no witch, just Lord and Lady Ernhardt.'

'She's a *witch*,' Jedka insisted. 'My mum says so. Mum says Lady Ernhardt is too beautiful so she must be a witch. She says we're all getting old and wrinkled but Lady Ernhardt has spells that keep her young.'

'She's right about us,' Olga sighed. 'But has your mother ever *seen* Lady Ernhardt?'

Jedka wasn't sure about that. 'My daddy has though. He sees her every day.'

Olga didn't argue with that. Instead she declared that school was over for today and the children hurried off to play, or to help their parents in the fields.

'I should go up to this castle,' the Doctor said

31

thoughtfully. 'Check they don't have any irradiated metal up there.'

'I've never been inside the castle either,' Olga said. There was a wistfulness in her tone. 'But they wouldn't have bought jewellery from Vadim. Well,' she corrected herself, 'I suppose some of the guards might. They drink in the tavern sometimes, and get meat from Drettle.'

'They might have found some of the same metal...' the Doctor said thoughtfully. 'Depends how far it was scattered.'

'The Watchman might have some,' Olga admitted. 'Where did it come from?'

But the Doctor didn't answer. In fact, he wasn't even listening. He was staring up at the clouds. It looked like rain. But then, it always looked like rain. 'Then there's poor Stefan,' he said. 'And the Plague Warriors.'

'You don't believe in Plague Warriors, do you, Doctor?'

'No, of course not. Not really. Not as such... But something killed Stefan.'

'And the others,' Olga said.

'Where did you say he was found?'

'In the churchyard.'

'But exactly precisely where?'

Before she could answer he spun round in a full circle, catching her by the arm to steady himself as he came round the second time.

'*Others?* What others? You mean, Stefan wasn't the first?'

The Doctor sat at the same table in the corner of the tavern. Klaus and Old Nicolai sat opposite the Doctor and Olga.

'There were always victims of the Plague Warriors,' Old Nicolai said. 'Even when I was a lad, my father told me to watch out for them. He'd lost a dog to the Plague Warriors. It turned up mutilated – ripped apart. Wolves, I thought.'

'That's more likely,' Olga said. 'Though the wolves seem mostly to have gone from the valley.'

'You hear them at night sometimes,' Klaus said. 'Never see them any more, though. Just as well.'

'But – other *human* victims?' the Doctor prompted. 'People. Dead people. Like Stefan.'

Nicolai took a swig of his drink. 'Plenty of them. But like I say, over the years.'

'Last one was last summer,' Klaus said. 'Gregor found him out in the fields, missing an arm and a lot of blood.'

'Dead?' the Doctor asked.

'Oh, he was dead all right.'

'Any ideas, Doctor?' Klaus asked.

'Lots. I'm full of them. Mr Ideas, that's me. But none of them very pleasant. I wonder…' He stared across at the counter where Gustav was washing up tankards. 'I wonder if he does mango juice and

33

lime. With ice. Lots of ice. Ice is… cool.' He frowned. 'Kind of obvious, that – sorry.'

There was a pause while the Doctor established that Gustav did not stock mango juice, and in fact had no idea what a mango was. Or a lime. And that if the Doctor really wanted to put ice in his drink then he was welcome to wait until winter then go and break up the frozen puddles that formed in the tavern's backyard.

When the Doctor returned, he explained what he wanted. Klaus looked pale, and drained his own drink in one gulp.

'I've spent all morning digging a grave for Magda. Won't be long before her husband needs one too.'

'Prolonged exposure in close proximity,' the Doctor murmured. Louder, he said: 'So digging up just one more grave should be easy then. It's been dug before, so the earth will be loosely packed. Easy. Piece of cake. Not actual eat-it cake, obviously. But, you know.'

'Just so you can see where we found Stefan, lying at the bottom of a pit he'd dug for Liza Clemp's body, God rest her soul.'

'And this Liza woman,' the Doctor said, 'she died of the plague too?'

'The poison,' Olga corrected him.

'The poison. Exactamundo.' The Doctor's face crumpled. 'Sorry – forget I ever said that.'

'What about Liza?' Nicolai asked.

'While we're digging up her grave, I might as well take a look at her body. Second opinion, sort of thing.'

'She died of plague,' Klaus said. 'Poison. Whatever.'

The Doctor nodded. 'Best to be sure, though, eh?' He finished his drink. 'Count her limbs, just to be on the safe side. Make sure they're all present and correct. Dead, obviously, but present and correct. Right, I'm all set. You got your shovel?'

The Doctor was right. It was easier excavating the recently dug earth. Klaus made quick progress. When he got tired and took a break, the Doctor removed his jacket, rolled up his sleeves, stretched his braces, spat on his hands, and took over.

'It's like sandcastles,' he declared, throwing another shovel-load of earth onto the growing pile beside the grave. 'Only more morbid.'

Klaus took over again, and finally his shovel hit wood. He scraped the soil away from the top of the coffin.

'We've been keeping Erik busy, if nothing else,' Olga said. 'He's the undertaker.'

The Doctor nodded. 'And they say it's a dying business. Sorry,' he added in the silence that followed. 'Was that in bad taste? Because, you know, it might have been.'

As he spoke, there was a creak from the grave.

Then a loud crack, followed by Klaus swearing.

They peered over the edge to see Klaus standing on the coffin lid. Except that one of his feet had gone through it.

'Skimps on the cabinet-making, does he?' the Doctor asked. 'Erik, I mean?'

'We've got a problem,' Klaus said, pulling his foot out. He looked as if he might be sick at any moment.

'Don't worry,' the Doctor told him gently. 'We'll just get a new lid. It's probably got a lifetime guarantee. Sorry,' he added, 'did it again there, didn't I?'

'It's not that,' Klaus said. He reached up so that the Doctor and Nicolai could pull him out of the grave. 'The coffin's empty.'

'But we only buried her yesterday,' Nicolai said. 'The grave wasn't disturbed.'

Olga was white. 'Walking dead.'

'You said yourself, that's just a story,' Klaus chided.

'Rapid decomposition,' the Doctor said. 'Is it possible? Can't be from the radiation.'

He jumped down into the grave, landing with both feet square on the remains of the coffin lid. It shattered beneath him, crashing through into the base.

'No,' the Doctor announced. 'She's definitely gone.'

He shifted his weight, kicking aside the shattered

wood. The bottom of the coffin was also broken, holes punched through the board and the slats splintered and torn apart.

'Hang about,' the Doctor said. 'This has been broken *into*, not out of. From below.'

His last word became a 'Woah!' as his foot disappeared through the bottom of the coffin, most of his leg following. 'Well, that answers that.'

'What answers what?' Klaus asked. 'You're making no sense.'

The Doctor struggled to free his leg, kicking off a section of wood that had attached itself round his ankle.

'There's a hole under the grave. Either Stefan dug right down to the roof of some cave or someone tunnelled in from below. Or possibly both.'

'Someone tunnelled into a *coffin*,' Nicolai said, 'and stole a whole *body*?'

'But who would do that?' Olga asked.

'Whoever stole Stefan's leg,' Klaus said.

The Doctor looked up at him approvingly. 'You know, you're not as daft as you look.'

'He doesn't look daft,' Olga said. 'I've never thought you looked daft,' she told Klaus. 'Not ever.'

'Right,' the Doctor decided. 'Well, I'll just take a look down here in this tunnel and see where it goes. There might be clues. I love clues. Clues are good. Useful things, clues.'

'Not now, Doctor,' Nicolai said.

'Yes, now. No time like the present. Though actually, if you think about that for just a moment…' His voice tailed off. 'How do you do that? It looks like there's loads of you up there suddenly.'

'Not now, Doctor,' Nicolai said again. 'You need to come up here. These men are from the castle.'

Klaus and one of the men from the castle reached down and helped the Doctor out of the pit.

There were two of them. They wore heavy jerkins with chain-mail vests over the top. Each had a sword strapped to his hip. They both had the weary, resigned expressions of men who had been in battle. Neither of them looked friendly.

The Doctor looked round, nodding happily. 'So, you're from the castle? I was going to come and visit later. Do I need a ticket or is it free admission?'

'Lord Ernhardt wants to see you,' the larger of the men said.

'Great. Super. As soon as I've finished here…'

'He wants to see you *now*.'

The Doctor stepped up to the man. His eyes were level with the soldier's chest. 'I'm busy *now*.'

'Doctor,' Olga said.

'Yes?'

'Maybe you should go with them. The tunnel will keep for later.'

'Whatever has happened to Liza,' Nicolai added, 'we can't help her now.'

'True enough.'

The Doctor turned back to the chain-mail-clad chest. 'So what's he want? This Lord Ernhardt – why's he want to see me?'

'You're a doctor.'

'True.'

'Lord Ernhardt's son is ill. He might have the plague.'

The Doctor sniffed, and looked up into the man's face. It was weathered and stern, craggy like it was fashioned from old granite, but there was a kindness lurking in the eyes.'

'You got children?' the Doctor asked.

'A daughter.'

'Do you love her passing well, as Hamlet might have asked?'

'I'd die for her.'

The Doctor nodded. 'You know, if you'd said "I'd kill for her" I'd be staying put.'

'But you'll come.' It wasn't a question.

'So long as I can bring a guest.' He turned to Olga. 'You said you'd never been inside the castle. Well, now's your chance.'

'Just so long,' Klaus said quietly, 'as she gets out again.'

Chapter 3

The castle was built into the valley wall as it rose steeply towards the black sky. It looked as if it had been hewn from the solid rock, and perhaps it had. The storm broke when they were halfway up the cliff path.

Lightning cracked the dark sky into pieces. Thunder echoed off the valley sides. The rain was instantly torrential, as if some great storm god had simply switched it on.

The two guards seemed unimpressed. They were obviously used to storms. Olga pulled her ragged coat tighter. The Doctor turned his face upwards to watch the rain rodding down towards him. He opened his mouth and closed his eyes.

'Refreshing!' he yelled above the sound of the

water hammering into the rocky ground. His hair was plastered to his forehead and his jacket was wringing wet. But he laughed and splashed in the puddles, and ignored the bemused stares of the guards.

'Sorry,' he said after a while. 'I guess you're all used to it.' He paused to let a particularly loud roll of thunder die away. 'But I haven't seen rain like this since last time I was in Great Yarmouth. Between you and me,' he said quietly to Olga, 'it's more like "Quite Good Yarmouth" these days. But don't tell them. It would take *so* long to change all the road signs.'

Water was running down the path and cascading over the edge. As they approached the castle, the Doctor realised that the cliff into which the castle was built was separate from the one they were climbing. Between the two was a chasm, perhaps twenty metres wide. Across it a narrow bridge led to the castle's main entrance. The bridge was a solid stone walkway, with no walls or railings. Stray off the path, and your next step would take you a hundred metres straight down to the rocky valley floor below.

Olga stayed right in the middle, as did the guards. But, fascinated, the Doctor sauntered to the very edge of the bridge and leaned out, looking down. He watched the rain tumbling away from him, and splashing into the valley.

'Makes your feet go sort of fizzy, doesn't it,' he called to the others. But perhaps his words were lost in the noise of the storm as no one answered.

The castle loomed above them. The gateway was twice the Doctor's height. As they approached, the larger guard, whose name the Doctor had discovered was Caplan, called out. With a clanking of heavy chains and the grinding of some ancient mechanism, the thick wooden door that filled the entranceway was hoisted up to allow them through.

Another guard stood beside the opened gate. He nodded to Caplan, who ignored him, and led his group inside.

The feeling that the whole structure might have been hewn from the valley wall continued. The inner courtyard was like a huge cavern, roofed with unbroken sand-coloured stone. Darker veins looped through it like beams. The whole place was lit with firebrands that burned smokily in holders on the walls.

'Are we impressed yet?' the Doctor asked Olga.

Like him, she was looking round in awe. She nodded silently.

'Good, isn't it?' the Doctor agreed. 'Do we get a guided tour?' he asked Caplan. 'I love guided tours.'

'Lord Ernhardt is waiting for you,' Caplan grunted. 'You watch your tongue while you're with him.'

'Watch my tongue?' The Doctor stuck his tongue

out as far as he could, shoving his chin out, and turning his eyes to look as far down as possible. 'Not sure I can see my tongue,' he said – rather indistinctly as he was still sticking it out.

'You'll see it all right,' Caplan growled. 'When Lord Ernhardt orders me to cut it out. I'll make sure of that.'

'May have to pass on the guided tour then,' the Doctor said quietly to Olga.

Caplan escorted the Doctor and Olga through a door, and down a passageway until they reached another door.

The room beyond was more like the drawing room of a great country house than the inside of a rock-hewn castle. The stone walls were softened by tapestries and large paintings. Several well-worn armchairs and a large sofa were arranged around a polished wooden table in the centre of the room.

Again, the room was lit by burning wall lights. A fire crackled in a large grate surrounded by a stone fireplace.

Olga looked round in astonishment, and the Doctor guessed she had never seen such opulence.

'How the other half lives,' the Doctor told her.

He had assumed the room was empty, so the reply surprised him.

'And which half do you belong to?'

The voice came from an armchair facing away

from them. Now that he looked, the Doctor could see a gloved hand holding a glass of amber-coloured liquid resting on the arm of the chair. Whoever was sitting there made no effort to get up or look round at them. So the Doctor and Olga walked round the other chairs until they could see him.

'Lord Ernhardt, I presume?' the Doctor said.

The man in the chair smiled, and raised the glass in confirmation and greeting.

'I don't care for people who presume... Not generally. But in your case, I shall be glad to make an exception. Thank you so much for coming, Doctor.'

'I didn't realise I had a choice.'

Lord Ernhardt leaped to his feet. He was tall and wiry, with thin features. His hair had turned to grey and, despite his being well into middle age, was still thick and well kempt, cut off the collar. He wore a long, dark jacket with an emblem like a stylised star sewn over the breast pocket. He set down his drink on a side table and reached out to shake the Doctor's hand.

'My dear Doctor, I am so sorry. I told Caplan to ask you if you could spare me some time. He does rather over-interpret his duties, I'm afraid.'

Lord Ernhardt's grip was powerful, even through the black velvet. The Doctor noticed with surprise that his other hand was ungloved.

'And unless I am mistaken, this is our excellent teacher, Miss Olga Bordmann.' Lord Ernhardt took

Olga's hand and raised it to his lips. 'A pleasure. I have heard such good things about you.'

Olga blushed with embarrassment, and even hinted at a curtsy.

'Several of my servants have children who have attended Miss Bordmann's school,' Ernhardt told the Doctor.

'Hardly a school, really,' Olga said apologetically. 'If they leave able to read a little and write their own names, it's something.'

'You are too modest,' Ernhardt proclaimed. 'I am sorry I'm not more involved in local affairs, but my duties often take me far away from here, to Malkeburg and beyond. When I am here, poor Victor consumes much of my time. If he were not so frail I might well have sent him to you for schooling, Miss Bordmann. As it is, his mother and I do what we can.'

'And you think he has the plague?' the Doctor prompted.

'He has a wasting disease of some sort. He has suffered with it for years.' Lord Ernhardt sighed. 'My Watchman does what he can, but recently the poor boy has deteriorated.'

'You think I can help?'

'To be honest, I doubt it. Oh, I don't mean to disparage your abilities, Doctor. But I'm sorry – I'm forgetting my manners. Can I offer you a drink? And you look soaked through, come and warm yourselves by the fire and tell me how things are in the village.'

Lord Ernhardt seemed as happy to listen as he was to talk. He enquired after the children that Olga taught – knowing several of them, including Jedka, by name and asking how they were getting on. Before long, she had almost forgotten where she was and who she was talking with. The Doctor too was easy company. She had not felt so relaxed in a long time.

After what seemed only a few minutes, but was probably much longer, Lord Ernhardt checked the time on a pocket watch and sighed apologetically.

'I really should look in on Victor. His mother is with him. Perhaps I can persuade her to leave him for a while. She gets so she forgets to eat or sleep…'

'May we see the boy?' the Doctor asked.

Ernhardt smiled. 'I still think of him as a boy but he is a young man really. Or would be…'

The passageway was chiselled into the side of the valley. According to Ernhardt, there was a vast maze of tunnels and passages behind and beneath the castle. 'Even I have not explored them all,' he confessed. 'My grandfather tried to map them, but I fear he barely scratched the surface.'

Burning torches were fixed to the wall, and Ernhardt also carried an oil lamp.

On the way, the Doctor explained about the jewellery and the radiation poisoning.

'So far as I know, no one here in the castle has any of this metal, Doctor. But I'll make sure that any there is gets collected up for safety. I suppose it's possible that Victor has been exposed to this poison,' Ernhardt conceded. 'But he was always a sickly child. I suspect his frailty derives from a different source entirely. He was born too soon. His mother almost died, you know. It was only the skill and diligence of – but here we are.'

They had arrived at a door set into the solid rock.

'It's a long way from the main living area,' the Doctor said as Ernhardt gripped the door handle with his gloved hand.

'The noises of everyday living disturb poor Victor.' Ernhardt pushed open the heavy wooden door with ease. 'Down here it is quiet. And I think he feels safe somehow, embedded in the heart of the mountain.'

Apart from the stone walls, the room was like an ordinary bedroom. It was more opulent than any bedroom Olga had seen before, but the arrangement of bed and side cabinets, with a trunk at the end was hardly unusual. It was a large room, with a vaulted stone ceiling, and the few pieces of furniture – a wardrobe, chest of drawers and several chairs – were lost in it.

Victor Ernhardt lay sleeping in the bed. The covers were drawn up to his neck. His face was pale and drawn, almost emaciated. But his father's features were echoed in the young man's. Sitting in a chair beside the bed, her hand resting on the covers over the boy's chest, was a woman.

She was, Olga thought, the most beautiful woman she had ever seen. Her skin was pale, but like porcelain. Her features too were delicate, her long fair hair immaculately combed out. She wore a simple green dress that seemed to emphasise how extraordinary she looked. But when she turned to see who had come into the room, there was a deep sadness in her eyes.

Lord Ernhardt hurried over, taking her spare hand between both of his own.

'There's no change,' she said.

'There never is,' Ernhardt said gently.

The woman was looking past Ernhardt. Her expression did not change as she stared at the Doctor and Olga. 'Who are these people?'

Ernhardt apologised and introduced them. 'And this is my wife, Marie.'

Olga stared back in surprise.

The Doctor voiced her thoughts: 'You can't be Victor's mother.'

Lord Ernhardt drew in his breath sharply. But his wife seemed unmoved. 'You think I am too young?'

'Well yes. Sorry – I didn't think it was rude to say a woman looked too *young*.'

'It is rude to suggest they are not the mother of their own child.'

'You *are* his mother?' Olga said, her surprise getting the better of her discretion.

'She is,' Lord Ernhardt said sternly. 'My wife is blessed with the appearance of youth.'

'To some,' the young-looking woman said quietly, 'that makes me a witch.'

'Not to us,' the Doctor assured her. 'People being older than they look is perfectly fine with me.' He grinned broadly.

Marie Ernhardt nodded. 'You are a doctor?'

'Yes.'

'A physician?'

'Ah. No. Actually. Though I read a lot.'

'I warned you not to get your hopes up,' Ernhardt said.

'I have very little hope left,' she told him. 'My hope is dying in that bed.'

'I can take a look,' the Doctor offered. 'I may be able to suggest something.'

'No!'

The door slammed shut.

'I absolutely forbid it.'

Standing by the closed door was a small white-haired man wearing wire-framed glasses. He peered angrily over them at the Doctor. Olga took a step backwards, but the Doctor stood his ground.

'Things that are forbidden are always so much more enticing, aren't they?' the Doctor said. 'Almost an invitation. You're talking to someone who sees

"Keep off the Grass" as a challenge.'

'I'm sorry, Doctor.' Lord Ernhardt seemed to have deflated. 'If the Watchman will not allow it…'

'Oh – so you're the famous Watchman. What do you watch?'

'At present, the sick and the dying. You are a doctor?'

The Doctor's eyes narrowed and he folded his arms. 'I'm many things. Why won't you let me help?'

The little man approached the bed. Marie Ernhardt moved aside to let him look down at her son.

'I have tended young Victor since he was born, since he first became sick.' There was a surprising tenderness in his tone. 'I cannot allow anyone else to treat him before my work is complete. You do see that, Doctor?'

'Honestly? No.'

The Watchman sighed. 'Then I'm sorry. Please be assured that I am doing what I can for the boy.'

'If anyone can save him,' Lord Ernhardt said, 'then it is the Watchman. He saved…' Ernhardt hesitated. 'Others. He has skills that ordinary physicians, even you, Doctor, can only dream of.'

The Doctor sniffed. 'I doubt that. I have the most extraordinary dreams. And if you ever meet my nightmares… Well, let's hope that never happens.'

'I have work to do,' the Watchman announced. 'I cannot concentrate if you insist on gossiping.'

'Gossiping?' the Doctor said. 'Gossiping?! I do not gossip. If you want to hear gossip you need to listen to Sir Thomas de Rosemont – now he could tell you a thing or two.'

'Doctor…'

Lady Ernhardt took his arm and led him gently to the door. Her husband and Olga followed.

'We must let the Watchman do his work.'

'He requires peace and quiet,' Lord Ernhardt explained. 'His work is very… delicate.'

'Why – what's he do?'

They were out in the corridor now. Lord Ernhardt pulled the door shut behind them.

'I don't know,' he confessed. 'But we have to trust him.'

'Why?' Olga asked. 'Why do you trust him?'

'Because he saved Marie here from the fever, many years ago. When Victor was born.'

'He is our best hope of saving Victor,' Marie Ernhardt agreed. 'We cannot upset him. I know you wish to help, Doctor. But your skills are unproven. We live with the evidence of the Watchman's craft each and every day.'

'We cannot risk our son,' Lord Ernhardt added. 'I hope you understand that.'

'I'm beginning to,' the Doctor said. 'But are you certain it was the Watchman who saved your life?'

'What if the fever just passed?' Olga agreed. 'How could you know – who else has he treated?'

'Treated?' Lord Ernhardt looked away. 'You speak as if he were a physician or a surgeon.'

Olga and the Doctor exchanged looks.

'Then – what is he?' the Doctor asked.

'So many questions!' Lord Ernhardt was suddenly angry. He stepped away from them, and thumped his gloved hand into the wall of the passageway.

There was a shower of dust. The fist embedded itself in the rock. A lump of stone fell to the ground. Olga gave a cry of surprise and shock. The Doctor took a step backwards.

'Alexander – calmly,' his wife said. 'They just want to help.'

'I know. I know.' Ernhardt sank to his knees. He picked up the fallen lump of rock in his gloved hand – the same hand he had punched into the wall. 'But I fear that we are beyond help. Even the Watchman's…'

He raised his hand, examining the solid stone. Then slowly, almost casually, he clenched his fist. The stone cracked, then shattered into fragments.

'The Watchman can repair anything in his workshop,' Lady Ernhardt said. 'He will fix Victor. He must!'

Lord Ernhardt nodded. He straightened up and took a deep breath.

'I must apologise, Doctor, and Miss Bordmann. But you will appreciate Marie and I want only what is best for our son.'

'Of course we do,' Olga said. She nudged the Doctor. 'Don't we?'

'We'll leave you to it,' the Doctor said. 'But when you do need my help, which you will, then just ask.'

'Thank you.'

'We can find our own way out.' The Doctor turned to go. Then he turned back. 'That's an impressive trick, by the way. Thumping the wall. Crushing the rock.'

'Several years ago, I was attacked by a wolf. It took my hand.' Lord Ernhardt held up his arm. The black velvet glove was dusty-grey from the stone.

'The Watchman mended it,' Marie said. 'He can mend anything.'

'Anything except your son. Yes, you said.' The Doctor took a step towards them. It took him into the shadows between two of the wall lights. His face darkened. 'Why do you call him the Watchman?'

'Because that is what he does. Or what he did, before he came here to help us.'

'He was a guard?' Olga asked.

Ernhardt gave a short laugh. 'No, of course not. He wasn't *that* kind of watchman.'

The Doctor took another step, so he was standing right in front of Ernhardt. He took hold of the velvet glove. 'May I?'

'Of course.'

The Doctor pulled the glove from Lord Ernhardt's hand. Behind him, Olga gasped in surprise. But the

Doctor nodded as if he had expected what he saw.

Beneath the glove, Lord Ernhardt's hand was made of metal.

'You call him the Watchman,' the Doctor said quietly, 'because he makes watches. He's a clockmaker. He doesn't work with flesh and blood, he works with mechanisms.'

'I've never seen the like of it,' Olga said, staring fascinated at Lord Ernhardt's hand.

He clenched his fist. Tiny motors and gears whirred into life. Joints moved, metal sinews and intricate mechanisms flexed.

'No one has ever seen the like,' Marie agreed.

'I have,' the Doctor said. 'That is the hand of a Cyberman.'

Chapter 4

The passageways all looked similar to Olga, but she was pretty sure they were heading in the opposite direction from where they'd come with Lord Ernhardt.

'How far is it back to the courtyard?' she asked.

'No idea,' the Doctor said. 'We're not going back to the courtyard.'

'Oh?'

'Shortcut,' he explained.

'It doesn't seem shorter,' she said after a while.

'No. But then my shortcuts are often rather longer than the original route.'

Olga considered this. 'So why bother?'

They rounded a corner, and found a flight of spiral steps descending into the solid rock.

'It isn't the destination that's important,' the Doctor said, pausing to examine the walls. 'It's what you find along the way.'

'And what do you expect to find?'

'No idea. Exciting isn't it?' He turned to grin at her before continuing downwards.

'But – it isn't a shortcut at all, then, is it?'

The Doctor looked at Olga sympathetically. 'It'll save loads of time. But later on. Trust me.'

The stairs arrived in another passage, and the Doctor looked both ways before deciding to turn left. They walked on in silence for a while.

Eventually, the Doctor said: 'Ernhardt told us this whole side of the valley is a maze of these passages and tunnels.'

'Too many for his grandfather to map them all,' Olga remembered.

'I think they're even more extensive than that. Too many for several grandfathers.'

The Doctor was taking turnings, choosing side passages, and descending more stairways apparently at random. Olga had long since given up trying to remember the route they had taken.

'Are you lost?' she asked after a while.

'No.' The Doctor paused, turning to look back the way they had come. 'I just have no idea where we are, that's all.'

'Sounds like we're lost, then.'

'We've been descending. Slowly, but it's onwards

and downwards all the same. I reckon we're close to the valley floor now.'

'How can you tell?'

'Pressure in the ears. You feel it?'

'No.'

The walls of the passage they were in were pitted and cracked. Cobwebs hung from above them, glittering in the guttering light from the ever-present wall lamps. The Doctor batted the fragile filaments aside with his hand. The floor was uneven and strewn with dust and debris that had fallen from the roof.

'I don't think this passage leads anywhere,' Olga said. The further they went, the more claustrophobic she was becoming. It was hot and dry. The sooner she felt the fresh air on her face and tasted the rain, the better. 'Look at the state of it.'

'Well, exactly.'

'What do you mean?'

The Doctor took Olga's arm and pointed. 'The way that pile of rubble is arranged – and I mean "arranged". The scuffed dust. The general state of the tunnel walls. Someone's gone to a lot of trouble to make it seem uninviting, like there's nothing down here worth seeing.'

'Doctor, that may be because there is nothing down here worth seeing.' She tried not to sound too exasperated. 'No one else has been down here for years.'

'Really?' The Doctor put his arm round her shoulder. 'Then who lit the lamps?'

'I don't know,' Olga admitted. He had a point. 'Do *you* know?'

The Doctor nodded. 'The Watchman lit them.'

'You're guessing. It could have been Caplan, or another of the guards.'

'Dust on the man's shoes matches this passageway. It's very distinctive.' The Doctor paused to drag the toe of his shoe through a pile of dust. 'Quite distinctive anyway. That is, I think it's pretty much the same. Look – Lady Ernhardt mentioned he had a workshop, and I want to find it.'

'You think it's down here?'

'I think he works in secret, alone, so yes – down here... Somewhere.'

A few minutes later, the Doctor was proved right. The way he made nothing at all of this suggested to Olga that he was well used to being proved right.

The tunnel opened out into a wider area with several other tunnels leading off. Set in one wall was a large wooden door, braced with metal bands. The Doctor turned the heavy iron handle and heaved. The door didn't move.

'Locked?' Olga suggested.

'Secrets often are.'

The Doctor produced his metal wand from his jacket pocket and aimed it at the door. The end of the wand lit up, and there was a whirr and a click. When the Doctor tried the door again, it opened. He grinned and stood aside to let Olga go ahead of him.

Like everywhere else, the chamber beyond the door was lit by burning sconces of oil attached to the walls. The room was vast, dominated by a central wooden table. It was covered with dismantled machinery, with metal and glassware and tools. There was a barely a space on the table. A huge magnifying glass held in place by a metal frame gave a distorted view of half the room. Alcoves round the edge were curtained off.

The Doctor was at the table in an instant, like a child finding a pile of new toys. He made his way round the table, examining everything.

'Recognise this?' He held up a metal gauntlet. It looked exactly like Lord Ernhardt's artificial hand.

'So many things,' Olga said. She didn't understand any of it. 'Did the Watchman make all this?'

'Some of it,' the Doctor conceded. He dropped the glove and it thudded heavily back down on the table. 'But an awful lot of it is very old.'

'Then where did it come from?'

'Good question.' The Doctor continued his journey of discovery. 'Same place as the jewellery that isn't jewellery, I should think.'

Olga dropped the metal pipe she was holding. It landed on the table with a loud clang. 'Is it poisoned?'

'Ooh.' The Doctor looked anxiously over the

table. 'Even better question. Hadn't thought of that. Hang on.'

He took out his wand again and swept it across the bits and pieces. It clicked like it had before, but nothing like as angrily or loudly.

'No. That's a relief. All this must have been a good distance from the reactor core. The jewellery is irradiated because it was part of the main housing. You don't understand much of what I'm on about, do you?'

'No,' Olga agreed.

'That's all right. He smiled. 'Neither do I, most of the time. But things are becoming clearer.'

'Not to me,' Olga murmured.

'I wonder where he found it all.'

The Doctor picked up the metal gauntlet again, peering inside the open wrist. Over his shoulder, Olga could see a mass of cogwheels and gears.

'Interesting?'

'Oh yes. He's stripped out the organic material and substituted a clockwork mechanism.'

The Doctor put down the gauntlet and picked up another mechanism, a collection of levers and cogs attached to a sealed sphere with thin pipes coming off it.

'This looks like he was trying to use steam.'

The Doctor set down this mechanism too, and started round the edge of the room. He drew back the heavy, faded curtain across the nearest alcove.

Behind it was another wooden table – covered in dismantled clocks and watches.

'He didn't give up the day job, then,' the Doctor said. 'This is where it all began.'

Not interested in clocks, Olga went to the next alcove and drew back the curtain. Behind it was a larger table. Leather straps hung from brackets at the side. On another, smaller side table, was arranged a collection of narrow knives, thin metal spikes, and other sharp instruments.

'Perhaps he is a surgeon, after all,' the Doctor said quietly.

'You mean…?' Olga shuddered. Was this an operating table? Was this where the Watchman had attached Lord Ernhardt's new hand? What else had he done here?

'I don't like to think what I mean,' the Doctor said. He drew the curtain across again. 'But I've seen enough.'

'You know what all this is?'

'Oh yes. And I don't like it.'

'Where did it all come from?'

'That's what we need to find out. And then make sure nothing else gets recovered. If this is all he's found, then we're lucky. Very lucky.'

'What else do you think there is?'

The Doctor put his finger to his lips. 'Someone's coming.'

Olga listened, but she couldn't hear anything.

'Are you sure?' she whispered.

'As sure as eggs is eggs,' he whispered back. 'Quick – in here.'

The Doctor grabbed Olga's hand and they ran to the next alcove, pushing behind the curtain. A burning sconce illuminated the small area where they stood. There was a tall stone plinth beneath the sconce, the sort that might have a statue or a sculpture displayed on it. But a sheet was draped over the top, masking the shape of whatever – if anything – was there.

The sheet moved. Just slightly, but enough to make Olga gasp. She reached out gingerly to pull the sheet away.

But then she heard the door to the room open. The sheet moved again – just the draught from the opening door, she realised with relief. She joined the Doctor at the curtain, and together they peered out into the room.

Two people had come into the room. One was small and wiry – not the Watchman, but a younger man. His lank hair hung in dark, greasy coils from his head and he was rubbing his hands together as he backed away from the other figure. She recognised him at once.

At first, Olga thought the second figure was a grotesque, misshapen creature, hunched and huge. But as it made its ungainly way across the room, she realised it was a large man carrying another figure over its shoulders. As the man turned, Olga gave an involuntary gasp, quickly clamping her hand over her mouth.

The figure was carrying the body of a woman.

The Doctor glanced at Olga but his look was full of sympathy rather than admonition. 'You know her?' he whispered.

Olga nodded, biting her lip. Afraid to reply.

'Liza, the plague victim missing from her own coffin?'

She nodded again.

'What about the other two?'

The smaller man had drawn back the curtain from the alcove containing the operating table. The larger man was setting down Liza's body on the table.

'Worm,' Olga hissed.

'He looks the type,' the Doctor agreed.

'And the butcher.'

'Steady – she died from the poison, we know that. He didn't butcher her.'

'No,' Olga whispered. 'The little man is called Worm. The larger one is Drettle – the village butcher. He sells meat.'

'So I see.'

Their job apparently done, the two men were standing by the main table, shuffling uncomfortably.

'So where is he?' the big man – Drettle – demanded gruffly.

'I don't know, do I?' Worm's voice was a

contrasting whine. 'But the door wasn't locked so he can't be far away.'

'He could be hours.'

'No point in waiting then. We'll get paid.'

'We'd better.'

Their conversation continued out of the door and down the tunnel, fading into the distance.

As soon as the door closed behind them, the Doctor whipped back the curtain and hurried to inspect Liza's body. Olga hung back. She had no wish to look at the corpse. She was no stranger to the dead, but the sight of a body always made her shudder.

'Definitely radiation poisoning. Did she have a ring made from the material?'

'I think she might have done,' Olga said.

'There's considerable discolouration round the fourth finger here, look.'

'I'd rather not, if it's all the same to you, Doctor.'

'It's all the same to me, Olga. Maybe one of those two ghouls pocketed the ring. He'll get a shock if he did. Not all at once, but over the next few months or years if he hangs on to it.'

The room seemed airless and hot. Olga was finding it hard to draw breath. She tried to stay calm, tried not to think about the people who had died because they just wanted a bit of good luck or divine protection. Tried not to think about Drettle and Worm – or the noise poor Liza's body made when they slumped it down on the table. Or what the Watchman intended to do with her now…

'Can we go now?' she asked.

'Yes, we can go.' The Doctor straightened up. 'This stops now. Today. All right?'

Olga nodded. 'You can stop it? The death…' She gestured to the cluttered table, to Liza's grey body. 'All this?'

The Doctor opened his mouth to answer. But from across the room came the scraping sound of the door opening.

Olga stood frozen, alone in the room. The Doctor seemed to have vanished, and the door was slowly swinging open. She looked round desperately for somewhere to hide. She was too far from the nearest alcove – she'd never get there in time. Where had the Doctor gone?

'Down here!' a voice hissed.

Without thinking, Olga dived under the big table. The Doctor pulled her close to him, a reassuring arm round her shoulders.

The view of the room from under the table was curtailed. Olga could only see the Watchman's legs as he walked slowly across to the table. She prayed he wouldn't look underneath – why should he? Except the floor under the table was scattered with boxes and debris just like the top of the table. She didn't dare move in case she knocked against something. But what if he needed one of the boxes…?

The Watchman continued past the table towards the alcove where Liza's body lay.

'Good, good. They've done well.'

The Doctor leaned closer and whispered in Olga's ear: 'He talks to himself. That's never a good sign.'

Olga did not reply. She talked to herself almost constantly when the children had gone home and there was no one else to listen.

'Well, obviously *I* talk to myself,' the Doctor went on. 'But that's different.'

The Watchman's voice was pitched up, as if he thought someone else was in the room. 'We have another body, my friend. We should get started straight away, it's already beginning to putrefy. Plague victim by the look of her.' For the first time there was a hint of sympathy in his voice as he added: 'Not so very old, either.'

'If he *is* talking to himself,' the Doctor murmured, echoing Olga's thoughts. 'Or perhaps he's just raving bonkers. It happens.'

'So,' the Watchman went on, 'shall we make a start?'

The answer came from the other side of the room – a sibilant, almost monotone voice unlike anything or anyone that Olga had ever heard before. It was hesitant, laboured, as if whoever was speaking was in pain.

'People… were here.'

The Doctor's arm tightened slightly round Olga's shoulder.

'Worm and Drettle. They brought the body.'

The Doctor's grip relaxed again.

'No… Others.' The words sounded forced out.

'Impossible. No one else knows about this place. Unless… You saw them?' the Watchman demanded.

'I heard them.'

'Of course, you can't see anything, can you… So what did you hear?'

The Doctor motioned for Olga to follow him as he crawled along under the table, careful not to bump into anything. They made their way towards the side closest to the door.

'I heard…' the voice said, and there was a slight hesitation now. 'Checking data... I heard… *the Doctor.*'

In front of Olga, the Doctor stopped abruptly. He raised his head at the sound of his name.

And cracked the back of it hard into the table above.

'The Doctor,' the Watchman echoed, just as the equipment and machinery on the table jumped and rattled. 'And he is still here!'

Chapter 5

The Doctor shot out from under the table, pulling Olga after him. They ran for the door.

'Doctor!' the Watchman shouted after them. 'What are you doing? Come back here at once.'

The Doctor was tempted. He had a lot of questions that the Watchman might be able to help him with. But he wasn't sure he'd like the answers. If he'd been on his own, he'd have risked it. But he couldn't put Olga in danger. Who knew what weapons the Watchman might have recovered. And the Watchman wasn't alone, as they now knew. Slamming the laboratory door behind them, the Doctor headed off down the tunnel, Olga close behind.

'Wrong way!' she gasped. 'We came from back there.'

'Not going back to the castle,' the Doctor told her as they skidded round a corner.

'Then – where?'

They paused for breath.

'Your friends Drett and Wormall didn't come from the castle.'

'Worm and Drettle,' Olga corrected him.

'Really – are you sure? Anyway, they must have come from down here. Look – the lamps are lit, so this passage is used.'

'They could still have come the other way.'

The Doctor raised his eyebrows. 'Carrying a dead woman through the castle might just attract unwanted attention.' He frowned as a thought occurred to him. 'Unless Lord Ernhardt is in on it, of course.'

'You think he might be?'

'That cyber-hand of his… Could smash through the bottom of a coffin. Or strangle a gravedigger.'

Olga's eyes widened. 'You don't think…?'

'No, actually, I don't. But it's a possibility we can't ignore. For the moment – onwards!'

The tunnels sloped gently downhill. The lamps were fewer and further between as they made their way through the tunnels. There was damp in the air, and the walls became darker and slick to the touch.

'Deeper and deeper,' the Doctor said.

'I hope you know where we are,' Olga told him.

'No. But I'm pretty sure where we're going to end up.'

They passed junctions and turnings, open areas with other passageways off. But each time, the Doctor took the route that was lit.

'Even easier than following a piece of string.'

They seemed to have been walking for ever, when there was a noise ahead of them in the tunnel. The Doctor put his finger to his lips, and they moved forward slowly and carefully.

'What is it?' Olga whispered. 'Sounds like voices.'

They turned a corner, carefully peering round into the gloom. The lamps were few and far between. The nearest was guttering and spitting as it burned down towards the end of its reservoir of oil.

Further down the tunnel, two figures were making their slow way onwards.

'We've caught up with our bodysnatchers,' the Doctor whispered. 'They're obviously in no hurry. Let's follow them and see where they go.'

'Can't we just get out of here?' Olga asked.

'I suspect that's where they're heading. Let's see.'

The Doctor waited until the figures were a good way ahead, and almost out of sight. Then he stepped round the corner, gesturing for Olga to follow. He took her hand, and together they crept after Worm and Drettle.

The murmur of the two men's conversation drifted back down the tunnel, but it was impossible to make out what they were saying. Worm's almost constant whine was counterpointed by the gruff, abrupt responses from Drettle. They disappeared downwards as the tunnel sloped sharply away again, as if they were being swallowed up by the earth, feet first.

Following at a safe distance, the Doctor and Olga saw that the tunnel dipped down to a wooden door. They were in time to see it close behind the two grave robbers.

'We'll give them a minute, then follow,' the Doctor said.

'What's behind that door?' Olga asked nervously.

'You'll see. Tell me about the church.'

'The church?'

'You mentioned a legend, or someone did. Thunderstorm and lightning, very very frightening. Sort of thing.'

'It's just a legend,' Olga said. 'A story.'

'I love stories. Don't you tell the children stories?'

'Of course I do. But they're children.'

The Doctor was grinning in the half-light. 'Aren't we all, deep down? Or maybe not so deep, some of us. Anyway, you never grow out of stories. So – tell me.'

There was a storm, or so the story went. Quite how long ago it was supposed to have happened, no one knew. Storms were hardly unusual, but this one was. It was ferocious, clawing and sweeping its way across the valley like a ball of fire. So much lightning that it turned night to day.

The villagers saw it, high above them, before they heard it. Then there was an almighty clap of thunder, a roar of sound, as the lightning bolt tore through the sky.

No one was outside because the rain was already torrential. Lightning and thunder stabbed and echoed through the night. But the ball of lightning was something else – never seen before, and never repeated.

It struck the church tower, ricocheting into the main structure and ripping off the roof. Or so the story said. Then it burrowed into the ground behind the graveyard leaving nothing but scorched, bare earth.

When morning came and the rain eased, the villagers came out to inspect the damage. The church was the main casualty. The tower was shattered, the whole of the top sheared off. The church itself was missing most of a wall and its roof. What was left of the beams and timbers still burned. The ground was so hot where the lightning bolt had struck that no one could get near without burning the soles of their shoes.

'It was just a storm,' Olga said. 'And it's just a story.'

'Wrong on both counts. It wasn't just a storm, and

it's not just a story.' The Doctor grasped the handle of the wooden door. 'Ready?'

'I suppose so.' She wasn't. Olga had no idea what might be waiting for them the other side of the door. If she was lucky, it was just Worm and Drettle. But she had a feeling that would be nothing compared with what the Doctor thought he might find.

The door opened onto darkness. Blackness that moved and shimmered as if it was alive. The Doctor reached out and shoved it aside – and Olga realised that the darkness was just heavy material. A faded, dusty tapestry covering the doorway.

The other side really was dark. The Doctor's metal wand lit up, illuminating the area with a pale glow.

Olga almost laughed with relief when she saw that beyond the tapestry was just a room – just another stone-lined chamber. Rubble was strewn across the floor. Behind them the tapestry fell back into place hiding the door.

'Wait a moment,' Olga realised. 'I know where we are.'

The Doctor was nodding. He had the same sort of expression as Olga herself reserved for a child who was not especially bright but had made sudden progress.

The room joined the crypt. They were beneath the ruins of the church. Olga couldn't help looking at the stone table in the centre of the chamber. But it was bare – Stefan's body had gone.

'Do you think Worm and Drettle took Stefan as well?'

The Doctor shook his head. 'Too obvious. They work in the shadows and the night. They'd want him buried and out of the way before they take him.'

'So – where is he?'

'Buried and out of the way, I expect. Your friend Klaus didn't waste time digging another grave.'

'He's not—' She was going to say that Klaus wasn't her friend. But of course, he was. He always had been. She just hadn't thought of him like that before.

The Doctor led the way through the crypt. Light was spilling down the steps from the church above, and he put the glowing metal wand away again.

'Can we find Klaus? We should tell him what's happened. And Old Nicolai too.'

'Soon. First I want to go up the tower.'

'Why?'

'I like church towers. Church towers are cool. Especially this one,' he added. 'Draughty and cold with the top missing, I should think. Come on.'

The church floor had been cleared of debris decades before. On the rare religious occasions when it wasn't raining, the villagers gathered to worship in the ruins. Olga told the Doctor how beautiful the church could look, lit by burning torches held by the villagers. How amazing the singing sounded echoing off the broken walls.

At the back of the church, a flight of steps led up into the remains of the tower. Like the tower itself, they were broken off prematurely. Undaunted, the Doctor started up them. The remains of the tower still stood above the original height of the walls. The steps were surprisingly wide, curling up through the structure.

Holes had been ripped in the tower walls. Moss and ivy was growing in over the torn edges. The Doctor stared down through one, not apparently worried by the height. Olga stood behind him, grateful for the breeze on her face. A fine mist of rain sprayed in through the hole in the wall, refreshing and cool. It was dusk – they had been down in the tunnels for so long that night was falling. The lights were coming on in the village, tiny points of illumination in the distance.

Level with where the roof of the church had once been, the stairs opened onto a platform that had been a room. The wooden floor had mostly fallen away, but the beams were still intact, with the broken remains of the floorboards still attached in places. Arched windows were cut into the walls on each side. One had collapsed, the mullions giving way.

The stairs continued upwards, but the Doctor stopped. 'What's that?'

There was something against the far wall. It was difficult to make out in the fading light from the windows. It looked like something from the Watchmaker's table – a collection of metal components held together with curls of wire and piping.

'Interesting,' the Doctor pronounced.

Olga cried out as the Doctor took a step forward. She thought he was going to crash down through the floor. But he skipped onto a nearby beam. Then, arms out wide, he made a rapid but precarious journey across to another beam, before hopping onto a surviving section of floor close to the apparatus.

'Joining me?'

Olga shook her head. Her heart was thumping so loud she could only just hear him. The Doctor had his wand-thing out again and waved it at the metal and pipes and wires. Olga didn't believe in witchcraft, well not really. But she crossed herself just in case.

'Glorified lightning conductor,' the Doctor announced. 'I think. Though it's a bit complicated. I wonder what else it does. And who put it here.' He turned to stare across at Olga. 'Who put it here?' he demanded.

'I really don't know. I've never seen it. I've never even been up here before.'

'So who has?' he wondered.

'No one, so far as I know. It's not safe. You can *see* it's not safe,' she said as he skipped back towards her.

'Safe as houses. Houses that have been hit by a…'
His voice tailed off. He was looking past Olga, up
the next flight of stairs.

'What is it?'

'I thought I saw someone. In the shadows.' He
raised his voice to call: 'Hello? Anyone there? Is this
your lightning conductor?'

'Worm and Drettle?' Olga suggested.

'Too tall for Worm, too narrow for Drettle,' the
Doctor said quietly. He looked anxious.

It was contagious. 'Why are you whispering?'
Olga asked.

'Not sure. But maybe because I've just thought
what it might be, hiding in the shadows. They like
the shadows.'

She was genuinely spooked now. 'What like the
shadows?'

'Well, you know them…'

A patch of darkness on the staircase moved. It
detached itself from the others and stepped down
onto the landing in front of them.

'… as Plague Warriors.'

It was huge – as broad as Drettle, despite what
the Doctor had said. And taller than Klaus. The
last rays of sunlight glinted on the pitted, rusty
metal of its armour. The whole head was encased
in a helmet fixed with bracing struts on either side.
One of the struts was bent out of shape. The warrior
took another clanking step forward, reaching out

an arm. A human hand clenched and unclenched spasmodically.

Olga and the Doctor backed away. Olga felt the ground give way behind her. She cried out, then realised she had reached the top of the stairs.

'Should we talk to it?' she gasped.

'Doubt it would help.'

The warrior tilted its head slightly as if listening. A faint blue glow shone from inside the slit covering the mouth. A sound came out, but it wasn't words, more like a metallic rattle.

'Doubt it could reply. It's damaged.' The Doctor gently eased Olga down the first step. 'Still deadly dangerous, but damaged. Let's hope it's slowed him down a bit.'

They turned together and charged down the stairs, feet echoing on the stonework.

'It's just a man in armour,' Olga said as they ran. 'He might need help. He was in pain.'

'He doesn't know what pain is,' the Doctor told her. 'That's sort of the point. The pain of others, maybe, as a weapon or a tool. But his own pain? Not a clue.'

'Is he infected, with the plague?'

They reached the bottom of the stairs.

'They don't get sick or ill. Cybermen don't get plague. They *are* plague.'

'Cybermen?'

'Later!'

They ran hand in hand across the church towards the south door. But the shadows were alive. Something moved in front of them. Not a Cyberman, but smaller, and low to the ground. Olga was sure she heard it *growl*.

The Doctor changed course without slowing, yanking at Olga's arm, pulling her after him. They clattered down the steps into the crypt.

'We're trapped!'

'No,' the Doctor said. 'We get out the way we came in.'

They ran through the crypt. The Doctor pulled the tapestry back from the door.

'Back to the castle?'

'I know a shortcut.' He glanced back as he opened the door, and saw her expression. 'No, really. A proper real actual shortcut this time. Honest. Although,' he added, 'you may not like it.'

The only light came from the Doctor's sonic screwdriver. And for once, that was a good thing. They had taken a narrow side tunnel off the main passageway.

'Knew it'd be here,' the Doctor boasted.

'How?'

'Because I am just so brilliant.'

'No, I mean what is the reasoning behind the brilliant assumption?' Olga asked.

'There had to be a way through to the graveyard.

It's probably the remains of old burial catacombs – look.'

He waved the sonic screwdriver helpfully so that Olga could see better.

She didn't want to see better. The walls were lined with shelves hewn from the rock and earth. On each lay the bodies of the dead – decayed skeletons staring back at Olga through sightless sockets. Black holes where once there had been character and thought, love and passion... Now, nothing.

Some of the skeletons looked almost complete. Most were not. The remains had been scavenged or looted over centuries. Broken fragments of bones crunched underfoot.

'Cybermen use whatever they can get their metal hands on,' the Doctor said as they pushed through the narrow passage. Fleshless skeletal fingers clutched and tugged at Olga's clothes. She stared straight ahead, trying not to think about it.

'Then there are natural, indigenous scavengers of course,' the Doctor went on brightly. 'You know, wolves and suchlike.'

'Thank you.'

Something in her sharp tone seemed to give him the clue that he wasn't helping.

'Not far now,' he said instead. He stopped, licked his index finger and held it up. 'Yes – nearly there.'

There was light ahead now – a flash like lightning.

But *underground*? Olga fancied she could make out the smell of rain on the grass. She was sure she heard thunder. It must be her imagination – her mind playing tricks.

'Here we are.' The Doctor stopped.

'But, we're nowhere.' They seemed to have stopped in the middle of the tunnel. A crushed skull watched from the shadows, its jaw missing and one eye socket smashed open.

Another flash of lightning, right above them. Olga wasn't quite quick enough blinking her eyes shut, and saw the full horror of the bodies strewn either side of them. Some of them didn't seem so very old. Some of them, she was sure she recognised – at least, their clothes.

'They drag them down here and take what they need,' the Doctor said. 'Fascinating. But macabre – sorry.' He stuffed away his sonic screwdriver and laced his fingers together making his hands into a step. 'Give you a leg up.'

'A what? To where?'

'You want to get out of here?'

From somewhere behind them came an animal howl.

'Yes,' Olga said quickly.

She put her foot into the Doctor's cradled hands, and he boosted her up towards the roof of the tunnel. Now she could see the dark grey of the sky outside. There was a hole in the tunnel roof. She scrabbled for a handhold, pulling herself up and through into a pit.

By the time she had worked out where she was, the Doctor had somehow struggled through behind her.

Above them, a dark shape loomed out of the darkness, staring down into the grave. It was there for long enough for Olga to see it was a man – or man-shaped. Then it gave a strange grunt, and slipped out of sight.

'Hello, Klaus,' the Doctor said. 'How you doing? Did you miss us?'

He leaped nimbly up and out of the grave. There was a pause before he reached back to help Olga out.

'Sorry about that. I'm just going for a little walk, collect some stuff. Your friend here seems to have fainted. Look after him.'

Chapter 6

'It's just a precaution,' the Doctor assured her when he returned from his walk. He hadn't told Olga where he'd been.

Olga regarded the little round blue tablet with some wariness. 'A precaution against what, exactly?'

'There's absolutely no danger whatsoever.'

'Which is why you have given me this small round blue precaution.'

'I've got one too,' he assured her. 'Look. Yum.' He popped it in his mouth, swallowed, and tried to make it look like the tablet didn't taste absolutely horrid. Without complete success.

'You still haven't told me what it is.'

'Anti-radiation pill. Everyone will need one. I've got loads. Well, I think there's enough.'

'And there's no danger at all.'

'Might have exaggerated that just a smidgen. Though probably not. We collected up all the irradiated jewellery, but some people will already be affected.'

'And this will cure them?'

'It'll stop them getting any worse. Most of them. For some…' The Doctor turned away, staring across the tavern.

The place was empty apart from the Doctor and Olga. Klaus had headed home when he'd recovered from witnessing a dark figure apparently rising from the dead in the graveyard. Even Gustav had gone to bed. As the Doctor had pointed out to Olga, it was the middle of the night, after all. Or it had been. The Doctor had spent so long saying things that Olga barely understood that it was probably almost morning by now.

'So, what will you do now?' Olga asked. 'Give out your little blue pills and then go home?'

'Home?'

'You must have a home.'

'Ah – *home*. Yes. Got one of those all right. It's where I keep the little blue pills.'

'So you'll be going home, then?' Olga said. She tried to keep the disappointment out of her voice.

'Um, well…' He avoided her gaze. 'Sort of… not. That is, not as such.'

'You mean "no", then, do you?'

'Yes. I mean, yes it's no. If you follow.'

Olga frowned. 'Are you going to tell me what you're planning to do?'

'You think I should?'

She nodded. 'I think you should.'

The Doctor considered. 'All right, I'll tell you,' he agreed. 'But you're not going to like it.'

Klaus joined them as the sun rose. The best Olga could persuade Gustav to provide for their breakfast was dark, dry bread and milk. The milk was good. After the Doctor had finished eating (and belched impressively before declaring 'Manners!'), he showed Olga and Klaus a large paper bag full of the little blue pills.

'Just tell everyone they're Parma Violets,' he advised.

Olga and Klaus looked at him blankly.

'Or not. Whatever. Moving on...'

The Doctor told them to make sure everyone in the village got two tablets. One to be taken immediately, the other before bed.

'It's just a precaution,' he said, and Olga raised her eyebrows.

'And keep everyone away from the area where the metal was found that the Talismans were made from.'

'It's part of Gregor's farm,' Olga said. 'Nothing grows in that field behind the church anyway.'

'It's cursed,' Klaus said. He glanced at Olga. 'Or so they say.'

'Poisoned soil, like poisoned people,' the Doctor said. 'Best make sure everyone knows to keep away. The radiation will eventually decay, diluted by the rain – there's enough of that round here, after all. But for the next century or so I'd keep well clear.'

'What will you be doing?' Klaus asked. 'Are you leaving?'

'Yes and no,' Olga told him.

'My work here is done,' the Doctor said seriously. Then he sighed. 'Oh, how I'd love it if that was *true*. I've always wanted to say that. But sadly not. Busy busy busy, that's me.'

'But doing what?' Klaus wanted to know.

'Oh, stuff.'

'To do with the Plague Warriors,' Olga said.

'Well, sort of. Look…' The Doctor took a few moments to rearrange the plates and beakers on the rough wooden table. 'Imagine the plague – the poison – is like this bread. The loaf has shattered, which isn't beyond the realms of the possible as it's pretty dry and stale.' He banged it on the table a few times to prove his point. 'So crumbs have spread right across the village. Which is this table.'

He pulled the bread apart and scattered bits of it liberally over the table, and over Olga and Klaus too. 'Actually,' he admitted, 'it's not at all like this, but I've started so I'll finish.'

Klaus and Olga just stared.

'Now, we've gathered up all the crumbs. Or rather, you and the villagers have. Well done, everyone.' The Doctor waited. He nodded at Klaus. He sighed. 'Go on then.'

'What?'

'Crumbs.'

'Oh, right,' Klaus realised. And brushed the crumbs off the table into his palm before dumping them back on the Doctor's plate.

'Now then,' the Doctor went on, 'did you see what I did there?'

'You made a mess and got someone else to tidy it up,' Olga told him.

'Well, yes. Story of my life, actually. But also I *kept* some of the bread!' The Doctor raised the remains of the loaf in triumph. He grinned, took a bite, chewed. The grin faded.

'So?' Klaus asked.

'So I'm going to look for the rest of the bread.'

'Which is poisonous, yes?' Olga said.

For a moment it looked like the Doctor was going to spit out his mouthful of bread. Then his face cleared. 'Ah – no, not really,' he said. 'That's just the hypothetical bread, in the metaphor, the allusion. We're looking for the real… thing. OK?'

Olga looked at Klaus. They both shook their heads.

The Doctor sighed. 'It's only the reactor and its

housing that are dangerous. I'm looking for the rest of it. Whatever it is. It'll be perfectly safe,' he said.

'Good,' Olga said. 'Because I'm coming with you.' Her words surprised her almost as much as they seemed to surprise the Doctor.

'You are?'

'You'll need help.'

'Don't argue with her,' Klaus said. 'It never works. She always gets her own way, she's so stubborn.'

'I am not,' Olga insisted.

Klaus smiled. 'See what I mean?'

'I'm coming,' Olga repeated. 'You said it's not dangerous.'

'Well, not really. Provided we take precautions.' The Doctor held out the paper bag. 'Parma Violet?'

The Doctor seemed to take more than necessary pleasure in explaining to Olga that they should steer clear of the church in case the Plague Warrior – damaged or not – was still there. Something else was also lurking in the shadows, he explained. But he was rather vague about what.

It was only when they reached the churchyard that Olga realised why he'd told her this at all.

'You can't be serious.'

The Doctor shook his head. 'I am always serious.'

'Well, I already know you well enough to be sure that's not true.' Olga looked down into the grave. 'You really are serious, aren't you?'

'We need to get into the catacombs. Can't risk going through the church. The castle's too far away. This is the only other door.'

Olga just stared into the dark pit.

'I'll lower you down.'

'Thank you.' She didn't mean it.

A few minutes later, grimy and dishevelled, Olga followed the annoyingly enthusiastic Doctor down the same bone-riddled passageway as she had suffered the night before. Again, she did her best not to look too closely at the skulls and bones and skeletons. Tried not to imagine they were watching her every step of the way. Blank, empty eyes stared out of the blank, empty darkness.

The Doctor had borrowed a couple of oil lamps from Gustav. He held his steady, raising it to illuminate anything of interest – usually gruesome interest. Olga's lamp wavered and flickered nervously.

'You want to know what I think?' the Doctor asked.

'Not especially.' She knew he would tell her anyway.

He did. 'A long time ago, there really was plague. Bubonic, probably. It was very popular from the fourteenth through to the seventeenth century. Oh look!'

As if to reinforce his point, the Doctor moved his lamp over a shelf hewn into the side of the tunnel.

A rat stared back at him from the inside of a skull. Its black eyes glittered for a moment, then it turned and scurried out of sight. Olga caught a glimpse of its tail – long, segmented, leprous…

'So the Black Death came and went. The victims were buried down here, or in lime pits below our feet. Memories persist, and any unexplained or frightening death is attributed to the plague. Or if it's too bizarre to the Plague Warriors.'

'And what are the Plague Warriors?' Olga concentrated on what the Doctor was saying in the hope it would be marginally less grotesque than the surroundings.

'Well, once upon a time…'

'Another story,' she muttered.

'… Long enough ago that no one remembers when, but not so long that it's been completely forgotten, something arrived here. It burned through the night sky and fell to the ground.'

'You mean the lightning storm that destroyed the church?'

'Whose story is this?'

'My apologies, Doctor.'

The Doctor sniffed, chose a passageway apparently at random and set off down it. This tunnel was slightly narrower than the others and – mercifully – dead-body-free.

'You were saying,' Olga prompted. 'One dark and stormy night…'

'Exactly. Well put – very apt. One dark and stormy night, something crashed into the church. A spaceship.'

'A *space* ship?'

The Doctor turned and looked back at her. His face was thrown into sinister shadow by the light from the lamps.

'Sorry, I forget the context sometimes. A spaceship,' he explained. 'A ship that flies through the sky, between the stars. Trust me, they do that.'

Olga shrugged. Maybe it was just a story after all.

'Anyway, the spaceship crashed. It badly damaged the church and ploughed, if you'll forgive the metaphor, into the farmer's field. Feel free to insert your own mashed potatoes joke here.'

There was a pause during which Olga made no jokes at all.

'Anyway,' the Doctor went on at last, 'spaceship crashes into field. The reactor housing is shattered, but the reactor shuts down safely, which is a blessing.'

'Why?' Olga wondered, though she had little idea what he was talking about now.

'Because the remains of the church and all of the village are still here. Rather than a big smoking hole in the ground.'

She nodded. 'Go on.'

The Doctor took another turning. The tunnel widened into a large area with several other tunnels leading off. The Doctor pointed to each tunnel in turn, including the one they arrived from. Then he sat down cross-legged on the ground.

'Reactor housing shatters, and over the years the villagers find bits and pieces of it. The radiation levels decay over time, but it's still enough to be fatal. Sadly.'

'Like a plague.' Olga crouched down beside him.

'As you say. Cancers, fatigue, tumours, general ill-health. The greying of the skin...'

'But you have cured that now. We collected the metal pieces, and you gave us the blue tablets.'

'Oh yes. Well, probably. But we're now right at the end of the process. It sorts itself out in time.'

'That is true of most things,' Olga pointed out.

'I hope not.' The Doctor jumped back to his feet. 'Or I'd be out of a job... This way, I think.' He set off down another tunnel. Olga hoped he was keeping track of the way they'd come, as she was already completely lost.

'And the Plague Warriors,' she prompted.

'Cybermen. They were on board the spaceship when it crashed.'

'And one of these Cy-ber-men survived the crash? The one in the church?'

'I suspect more than one survived. They're scavengers essentially. They take what they need to survive whatever the cost. But in this case someone's been scavenging *from* them.'

'Who?'

In answer the Doctor held up his hand. They stopped, just shy of a sharp bend in the tunnel. 'Listen,' the Doctor whispered.

At first, Olga could hear nothing. Then she realised that what she had taken for a general background buzz in her ears was in fact voices. Distant, indistinct, but voices.

Gesturing for her to be careful, the Doctor peered out round the corner of the tunnel. Olga pushed past him, leaning out so her head was below his.

Ahead of them the tunnel opened out into a huge cavern. The sides of the area receded into darkness. But across from where the Doctor and Olga were, two figures crouched beside a pile of debris. They were lit by oil lamps, similar to the ones the Doctor and Olga had brought.

The debris glinted in the flickering light – metal and glass, plastic and rubble. It had spilled down into the cavern through a hole ripped in the side of the area, like a landslide at a rubbish tip. There was a faint red glow from beyond.

'Is that the sky ship you spoke of?' Olga whispered.

'Some of what's left of it.'

'And Drettle and Worm,' she said, nodding towards the two distant figures.

'Looks like they don't just loot bodies,' the Doctor said. 'Collecting stuff for our friend the Watchman, probably.'

'Like the items he had in his room, on his table?'

'Exactly,' the Doctor agreed. 'He makes use of whatever he can find. Like Lord Ernhardt's hand. Not good.'

'No?'

'Anachronistic,' the Doctor said, as if it was a swear word.

'What does that mean?'

'It means it shouldn't be here. Not here and certainly not now.'

Olga considered this for a moment. 'Are your precaution tablets also anachristics?'

'That's completely different. The evidence gets destroyed by the process of using it.' He pulled out his metal wand with his free hand. The lamp juddered alarmingly in the other. 'Talking of which…' He checked the readings. 'No, we're OK here. Level's not too high.'

'And what about those two?' Olga asked, meaning Drettle and Worm.

'Ignore them for now. We need to see that ship. Now we know where it is, we can circle round and find another way in.'

Olga was more inclined to circle round in an about-turn and head straight back home. Or at least towards daylight and the inevitable rain.

'What are these tunnels?' she asked as they turned down yet another passageway hewn from the living rock. It was more to take her mind off other things than because she really wanted to know. But once she had asked the question, she realised she was interested to know the answer.

'Mining originally, I'd think,' the Doctor said. 'Adapted in medieval times for catacombs and burial chambers.' He wiped his finger down a wall, examined the dust he'd collected, then licked it off. 'Iron ore, and the stone's obviously good for building.' He glanced up at the roof of the tunnel. 'It isn't natural.'

'Not if it was a mine,' Olga agreed.

'Oh I didn't mean the tunnels. I meant the weather.'

'Weather? Down here?'

'No, no – up *there*. All that rain. Lightning and thunder. It's worse than…' He paused, perhaps to think of the rainiest, wettest, stormiest place he'd ever been. 'The planet Karn. Or no, wait – Margate,' he decided. 'Worse than Margate. It definitely isn't natural.' He paused to grin at Olga, his face contorted grotesquely by shadows from the flickering oil lamp he held. 'Which is why we're here. Keep up.'

Olga wasn't sure if he meant keep up with his walking or his elliptical conversation. But she hurried after him anyway.

The ship from the sky had crashed through the walls of the tunnel, embedding itself in the solid rock. A wall of metal cut across their path. But the side had been ripped open by the impact, leaving a ragged tear through the bent, rusted side. From within the dark maw came a deep blood-red glow.

'Emergency lighting,' the Doctor whispered. 'Since the reactor was obviously damaged beyond repair, they must have long-term storage cells.' The Doctor's metal wand whirred and whistled. 'Fuel cells can only store power for a while, so they must be replenishing it too. Capturing it from the atmosphere, like using a lightning conductor.'

'That is the term you used for the device we found in the church,' Olga recalled.

'Well remembered. They're channelling the power from the lightning storms. Storing up energy they drain from natural phenomena.'

As he spoke, the Doctor was already climbing through the jagged hole. He turned back for long enough to add: 'Except of course, as we said – it's not a natural phenomenon.'

Olga followed the Doctor, keeping carefully clear of the sharp edges of torn metal.

He offered no further explanation, but set off into the red light. They were in a wide walkway. It joined a gantry, from where Olga could look down into deep red nothingness. 'I can't even see the ground below.'

'Ship's bigger than I thought,' the Doctor admitted. His voiced echoed off the metal walls. 'Lifts are probably out, but there should be emergency stairs.'

The gantry ended in a metal stairway leading steeply downwards. The steps were obviously intended for someone with far longer legs than Olga and she practically had to jump down each one. The oil lamp guttered, and she wondered how long it was going to last. She didn't fancy being plunged into near darkness, the world only lit blood-red. She felt chilled at the thought.

'We could dismantle the equipment in the church tower,' the Doctor said as he descended the stairs with ease. 'Assuming we could get past the Cyberguard and its mate.'

'Its mate? You mean like animals take a mate?'

'No. Animal definitely, but more of a pet. And that makes things tricky. Probably just one Cyberman left awake to sort things out. That'd be the efficient way to do it, and they're nothing if not efficient are the Cybermen.'

'And what is this one lonely Cyberman doing?'

'Slowly drawing off power to keep the ship alive. There may be others, held in suspended animation. Hibernating. Asleep. Preserving power and resources.'

'Others? How many?'

'Oh not many – just one or three. Whatever survived the crash.'

Olga jumped down yet another step. She shivered. After the stifling tunnels, it seemed cold down here. 'You say they are asleep. Hibernating.

Hibernating animals are revived by the warmth of the new spring. What if they wake up?'

'Not likely. They're drawing power from the storms, and like I said it's not natural – they're seeding the atmosphere to create the storms. But without a power converter, it's very inefficient. They're just using induction. Most of the energy gets lost again.'

'If you say so.'

'Oh yes, I do. This is me, here and now, saying it. I saw what's in the church, and the tail-end of this ship where Drettle and Worm were scavenging was shattered. That's where the power converter would be if they had one.'

'So the Plague Warriors will not wake.'

'That definitely won't happen,' the Doctor said confidently. 'Because for another thing, I saw broken bits of power converter on the Watchman's workbench.'

Finally they had reached the bottom of the steps.

'What's this place? Are we still within the ship from the sky?' Olga's voice echoed – the chamber was obviously large. 'It's freezing.' She held up her lamp. 'I can see my own breath – look.' Olga breathed out heavily by way of demonstration.

'Probably because there's no power and the heating's all switched off. It's below minimal lighting too. But since we're not worried about wasting the energy that the Cybermen think they're saving for their resurrection…' The Doctor set down his lamp on the floor and strode into the red-darkness. There was a 'thunk' as he threw a switch. 'Let there be light!'

Enormous lights flickered on high above them. At floor level too, lamps burst into white-brilliance. The polished silver walls reflected the light again, and after the near-darkness it was so dazzling that for a while Olga could see nothing.

She heard the Doctor's gasp before she could see what he was looking at. She blinked quickly, and gradually her vision cleared and she could look into the bright light.

The chamber they were in was huge – as large as her father had described the cathedral at Drettenburg, and as tall. The far wall rose high above them. A structure of metal walkways and gantries, similar to the ones Olga and the Doctor had already traversed criss-crossed the wall. It took Olga a moment to work out its purpose. Then she realised that the walkways connected to steps cut into the metal framework at either end of the wall so that the whole upright beam formed an enormous ladder.

Arranged along each walkway were hexagonal doorways, a honeycomb of tessellated cells. They looked tiny at the top of the wall, but closer to ground level, Olga could see how large they really were. Each doorway was covered with a translucent membrane, dusted with frost, like a thin layer of ice across the surface of a pond.

'I told you it was cold,' she said, putting her lamp down on the floor beside the Doctor's.

But the Doctor didn't answer. He was staring in horror at the structure.

'What is it, Doctor?' Olga asked. 'Are these storehouses of some sort? To preserve things the Plague Warriors may need on their voyage through the sky?'

'Sort of.' The Doctor's voice was a husky whisper. 'Certainly storage. This is a colonisation ship. They spend the journey inside those cells, frozen into immobility, preserving their power, conserving energy and resources. One inside each compartment. Dozens of them.'

Olga shivered, and not just from the cold. 'Dozens of what?'

'Cybermen.'

Chapter 7

'But they are hibernating, you said. And it is certainly cold.'

Olga seemed drawn to the honeycomb of survival cells.

The Doctor was also making his way slowly but inexorably towards the cells. 'On Telos, the archaeologists referred to these structures as the tombs of the Cybermen. But they never expected them to wake up again.'

Olga paused in mid-step. 'When spring comes – will they wake up then?'

'Not if I can help it. There's certainly not enough power right now, so we're quite safe.'

They had reached the tombs. So close, Olga felt dwarfed by the structure that rose high above her.

Her feet felt fizzy just at the thought of how high it was.

The Doctor reached out and brushed at the thin membrane over the front of the nearest compartment. Through the smeared frost and glittering ice, Olga could see a figure inside. It was curled up into a foetal position, but even so she could see its size, imagine its power.

'Those tombs you mentioned,' she said slowly. '*Did* the Cybermen wake up?'

The Doctor hesitated. 'I don't remember.'

'You are not a good liar.'

'It was a completely different situation,' the Doctor protested.

'Frozen Cybermen waiting to thaw. In what way was it different, exactly?'

'Well...' The Doctor looked round, brows furrowed as if he was hoping to see something that would provide a good answer to Olga's question. His face cleared. 'Well, for one thing, on Telos, they didn't leave a damaged Cyberman on guard.' He frowned. 'Though maybe that's not such good news right now.'

The Cyberman was tall – towering over even the Doctor. It was huge compared to Olga as it stepped out of the shadows at the side of the chamber. The metal of its armour was pitted and rusty. One of the struts from its head had snapped off leaving a jagged stump.

As it marched towards the Doctor and Olga, they saw that one of its arms had been torn off at the elbow. A mass of wires and cables fanned out from the joint, like the roots of some metal plant. But below the collar of wiring, a new arm was grafted incongruously in place. A pale, human arm with delicate fingers, nails broken and grimy. Some of the wires ran down the outside of the arm and looped over the fingers like a flexible metal cage.

The arm seemed out of proportion, short and slender, as if the metal armour had been stripped away to reveal the flesh beneath. Discoloured, rotting flesh.

Together with the Doctor, Olga sidled along the front of the tombs. The Cyberman stopped, looking at them almost quizzically, head slipping slightly to one side.

'It's all right – we'll see ourselves out,' the Doctor said.

The Cyberman didn't move or answer. It was as immobile and silent as a statue.

'Can it understand us?' Olga whispered.

'Not in a million years. It might be able to comprehend the words we use, but what we mean by them – the emotion and humanity of it? Never. Not sure what it's up to, actually.' The Doctor took a wary step back towards the Cyberman. 'Deactivated, maybe? If the power levels are low.'

'Take care,' Olga cautioned.

'No, it's all right,' the Doctor told her. He reached out and knocked his knuckles against the Cyberman's shoulder. It clanged like a hollow suit of armour.

The Doctor grinned and turned back to Olga. 'You see?'

But as soon as he turned away, the Cyberman was moving again.

'Doctor!' Olga warned.

The Cyberman's metal fist lashed out, snatching at the Doctor. The Doctor dived to one side, but the fist connected with his arm, knocking him sideways. The Doctor sprawled across the floor. The Cyberman leaned down to grab him.

Without thinking, Olga launched herself at the creature's back. It was like running into a stone wall. But she managed to knock the Cyberman slightly, so that its fist smashed down into the floor, missing the Doctor's head by a fraction. The sound of metal on metal echoed round the chamber.

The Cyberman straightened up, turning to see where Olga was. She jumped backwards, desperately trying to stay out of reach as it lurched towards her, arms outstretched.

Behind the Cyberman, the Doctor leaped back to his feet. He charged at the metal man, knocking it with his shoulder and sending it staggering a few steps sideways.

It was not off balance for long. But it was long

enough for the Doctor to grab Olga's hand. 'Come on!'

'Where to?' she gasped as they ran.

'Anywhere!'

It seemed much further back to the steps, as if the chamber had somehow expanded while the Doctor and Olga examined the tombs. The rhythmic thump of the Cyberman's steps followed them, gaining speed, closing in on them. The main lights cut out suddenly, and the whole place was again bathed with a pale, blood-red glow. The shadows pressed in around them.

The stairway was a mountain to Olga. The steps were so widely spaced that each was a struggle. The Doctor's long legs had no trouble. He still had hold of her hand, jolting her shoulder with every upward movement. When he paused to look back and see how she was doing, it was concern etched on his face rather than frustration. Olga forced a smile. The Doctor's eyes widened.

And a hand grabbed Olga's ankle. The Cyberman pulled her leg from under her and she crashed down face-first on the metal stairway. The breath was forced from her body so she couldn't even scream.

The Doctor leaped over her, landing with a *shhhunnk* on the Cyberman's wrist. The sound that grated out from the metal creature might have been pain, or anger, or just a mechanical response. But Olga heard the bone in the human arm snap. The pressure on her ankle was gone. She tore it free of the failing grasp, and hauled herself upwards.

'Lucky he didn't use his other arm,' the Doctor gasped as they hurried on up the stairs. 'I'd have needed a crowbar.'

There was no time to catch their breath. The Cyberman was already back on its feet. The human arm hung limply at its side, but it strode purposefully up after them. It moved steadily. Not as fast as Olga – who was spurred on now by pain, fear, and adrenalin. But she knew from what the Doctor had told her that it would never tire.

They reached the level walkway at the top of the stairs. Their running footsteps reverberated metallically round the chamber, counterpointed by the steady tread of the Cyberman. The sound seemed to come from all around them, echoing back from the other end of the walkway.

The Doctor skidded to a halt halfway along the gantry.

'What is it?' Olga demanded. 'Why have you stopped?'

'You hear that?' He was looking all round, peering into the gloom. Several metres below them, another walkway crossed underneath. Red light shone up through the mesh and ironwork.

The sound of the Cyberman's footsteps beat a regular rhythm. But there was a double-beat now for every tread.

'There is another one,' Olga realised with horror. 'But where?'

'That's what I was... Ah.'

The Doctor pointed along the gantry. The red light glinted on rusted metal ahead of them. Another Cyberman was making its way inexorably towards them. Olga turned quickly – to see the first Cyberman approaching from behind.

'Open to suggestions,' the Doctor said. 'Don't think they want to chat. In fact, one of them's after a new arm.'

Something in the way he said it told Olga exactly where the Cyberman would look for the arm. 'I would rather not think about that,' she said.

'Then think of what we do now.'

'Your metal wand?'

'The sonic screwdriver? Sadly, it doesn't do Cybermen.'

The two Cybermen were closing in. The metal floor under Olga's feet was shaking with their heavy footsteps.

'So what *does* it do?' she demanded.

'Ah, good point.' The Doctor took out the wand – the sonic screwdriver. He twirled it between his long fingers. 'It does bolts. So hold on tight!'

'Bolts? What do you mean *bolts*?'

'Actually, make that *very* tight.'

Just ahead of them, the gantry rail was jointed. One long metal strut was fixed to the next. The join, Olga now saw, was repeated with the walkway beneath her feet. The whole section they were standing on was fixed to the next – with large, weathered bolts.

Rust flaked from the bolts on the floor section as the Doctor aimed the sonic at them. The end flared into life, accompanied by a high-pitched whirring sound. Slowly, the bolts started to turn. The gantry jolted as the joints loosened, and Olga grabbed the side rail, hugging it tight under the upper arm, bracing herself against the inevitable fall.

With a scraping, grinding roar of protest, the whole section of the gantry ahead of them dropped away at one end. It tore free of the loosened bolts, collapsing onto the gantry crossing underneath.

The Doctor and Olga stared down.

'Ah,' the Doctor said. 'Right. Was kind of expecting the section *we* are on to fall actually. Then we could escape along there.'

'Instead we now have nowhere to go and an angry Cyberman approaching,' Olga said.

'No, no, no,' the Doctor chided. 'Not angry. They don't do angry.'

Beneath them, the Cyberman on the fallen section of gantry pulled itself to its feet and stared up impassively at the Doctor and Olga. The Doctor gave a little wave.

'I think, all in all, this counts,' he said, 'as an "Oops".'

They turned to face the other Cyberman, now just

a few steps away from them.

'Backs to the absence of wall,' the Doctor said. 'So only one option.'

Olga glanced behind her. She was perilously close to the broken end of the gantry. The Doctor took her hand. She held on tight, hoping he had a plan. *Any* plan. No matter how ridiculously dangerous and foolhardy.

Even so, she wasn't prepared for his next word.

'Jump!'

There was no time to object. Since Olga was holding tight to the Doctor's hand she had no choice but to jump with him as he leaped off the end of the gantry. The Cyberman below looked up at them through blank teardrop-sad eyes. If its eyes could have widened, perhaps they would have done as the Doctor and Olga dropped towards it.

The Doctor's feet hit first – connecting with the Cyberman's chest and driving it back against the gantry rail. The structure was already angled downwards where it had fallen. The combined weight of the Doctor and Olga sent the metal giant staggering backwards. Its arms lashed out as it tried to hold its balance. But the angled rail caught in the small of the Cyberman's back.

It pivoted round, over the rail, and crashed to the floor far below.

Face-down on the gantry where she had landed, Olga stared down through the mesh of the walkway.

The Cyberman lay on its back, crumpled and dented. One leg was bent round underneath it. The side of the head had been staved in by the impact. Dark fluid wept out of one misshapen eye…

She looked up, smiling at the Doctor with relief. But the expression froze on her face. Above them, the other Cyberman stood at the broken edge of the upper walkway. The Doctor hauled Olga to her feet as she realised what was about to happen.

'Doctor—'

'I know,' he said. 'Run!'

Olga gathered up her skirts and raced after the Doctor along the walkway, away from where the upper level had smashed into it. Behind them, the Cyberman jumped. The whole structure shook as the Cyberman landed, both feet together, on the walkway.

'Now what do we do?' Olga called as they ran.

'I had my go. Now it's your turn to think of something,' the Doctor yelled back.

The gantry connected to another stairway, which took them up to the level they'd been at before jumping down. Along another walkway, and they found themselves back in the main corridor.

'This way.' The Doctor charged off down the corridor.

'But we came in…' Olga sighed, glanced back to where the Cyberman was stomping after them, then ran after the Doctor. 'It doesn't matter.' Maybe – just maybe – he knew what he was doing.

At the next intersection they paused for breath. Not that the Doctor seemed to need it, but Olga certainly did.

'Where are we going?' she managed to ask between deep gulps of air. 'We came in back that way.' She nodded back the way they had come. In the distance, they could both hear the metallic tread of the approaching Cyberman.

'Did we?' the Doctor seemed surprised. 'Never mind, we'll sort something out.'

'Sort something out?!'

'Trouble is,' the Doctor went on, looking round and peering into the red gloom, 'I used to know the layout of a typical Cybership like the back of my hand.'

'What happened?'

He waggled his hands, fingers close to her face. 'Got new hands.'

She wasn't even going to ask about that. The Cyberman was getting closer again, so she grabbed one of the waggling hands and dragged him on down the corridor.

'At least it's not shooting at us,' he said happily.

'What?'

'Not enough power for energy weapons.'

The light was fading, and they charged on into darkness. The thump-thump-thump of the Cyberman's pursuit was ever present. Somewhere ahead was a faint glow. Not the ubiquitous red of the emergency lighting but a warmer, yellowish light.

'Can you tell where we are yet?' the Doctor asked. His teeth caught the light as he grinned.

The glow increased as they approached, running, hand in hand. The corridor seemed to open out ahead of them. The glow was coming from the far side, shining in through a hole torn in the wall.

'Cargo bay,' the Doctor said as they ran. 'Explains where all that stuff came from.'

'Stuff? What do you mean by "stuff"?'

They raced towards the hole in the side of the ship.

Too late, Olga realised that the glow was coming from below them. They were about to run through a hole in the side of the ship – high above the ground outside.

As they reached the broken wall, she saw where they were. The rocky cavern spread out ahead of her, its edges lost in darkness. The glow came from an oil lamp precariously balanced on a sloping pile of debris and detritus.

'Geronimo!' the Doctor yelled as he leaped out of the ship and clattered down the steep pile.

It was like running on a shingle beach. Olga's feet sank into the shifting debris. Every step was an effort.

A crash from behind them alerted her to the

approaching Cyberman.

Ahead of them, Drettle and Worm looked up in surprise. Their eyes widened as the Doctor staggered past, Olga close behind him.

'Don't just stand there, you two. Run!' the Doctor yelled.

The Cyberman was charging down the slope, wading through the debris. Components, circuit boards, broken metal, bent plastic, all shoved aside as it strode after its prey.

The smaller man, Worm, let out a yelp and rushed after the Doctor and Olga.

But Drettle seemed rooted to the spot. The Cyberman barely seemed to notice him. Its metal arm swung out in a savage chopping motion as it passed, and the big man was hurled backwards across the debris he had been sorting.

Olga watched, horrified. She had never seen a man killed before – and the casual manner of it froze her, numbing her thoughts. The Doctor grabbed her by the shoulders, turned her round, and pushed her onwards.

'It's too late for him. I'm sorry, but there's nothing we can do now except save ourselves.'

The Doctor and Olga's lamps were still back by the Cyber tombs where they'd set them down after putting on the main lights. Worm and Drettle's lamp toppled over, and went out. The only light now was a pale red glow from the side of the spaceship.

Ahead of Olga, Worm was racing for the nearest tunnel – where the Doctor and Olga had watched from earlier. But there was something moving in the gloom. A guttural roar split the air.

Worm skidded to a halt. He looked back at the Doctor and Olga – and the Cyberman behind them. Worm's eyes were wide, his mouth open in a silent scream of horror.

He turned back towards the sound. Out of the darkness came a mass of fur and teeth. It had metal jaws, a head braced with a metallic cage, legs augmented with hydraulics, and paws tipped with claws of sharpened steel.

The Doctor and Olga pulled up as the creature bounded towards them. Behind it, came another one. And a third behind that.

'The good news is – now we know what happened to the wolves,' the Doctor said quietly.

Chapter 8

The Doctor swerved in mid step, pulling Olga with him. Worm was closer to the approaching cybernetic wolves. It was too late for him.

The first wolf leaped with a hydraulic hiss and an animal roar. Metal teeth clamped round Worm's throat. He screamed and fell. The second wolf joined the first, ripping into the man's body with its teeth and claws.

The last of the wolves kept running – bounding after the Doctor and Olga as they raced for another tunnel entrance. Olga imagined she could feel its hot breath on her back. She risked a look over her shoulder, and saw with relief that they were still well ahead of the wolf. But it was gaining on them, and the Cyberman too was coming after them. She caught a glimpse of Worm, lying in the middle of the cavern, the two cyber-wolves still at his body. Feeling suddenly sick, she turned away.

The tunnel was a gaping dark hole in the side of the cavern. The Doctor fumbled in his pocket for the sonic screwdriver as he and Olga plunged into the blackness.

'Can those creatures see in the dark?' Olga gasped.

'I'd be surprised if they can't,' the Doctor told her. 'They live in the shadows and the darkness, like I said.'

She didn't know whether he was talking about the wolves or the Cybermen. Either… Both.

The end of the sonic screwdriver glowed, bathing the tunnel ahead of them with a sickly pale light.

'Are we faster than them? Are they following?' Olga demanded. 'Where are we going? Are we lost? Will we ever get out of these tunnels alive?'

'No, probably, not sure, absolutely not, and I hope so.'

'What?'

'Well – you asked.'

They turned down a side tunnel, clattered past a skeleton resting on a ledge, and on into another, wider tunnel.

'And you are sure that this is the right way?'

'Sure,' the Doctor told her. 'I'm taking a sort of objective-based approach to this.'

'What objective is that?'

'To get as far away as possible from anything that wants to kill us.'

Olga couldn't tell if the Cyberman was still after them. But she could hear the wolf's cries echoing down the tunnel. Was it getting closer?

'I think it has our scent,' she said.

'Scent, of course.' The Doctor spun round, holding the wand out in front of him like a sword. It whirred and glowed even harder.

'What are you doing? You hope to dazzle it with bright light?'

'Not a bad idea, actually. But no. I'm agitating the air molecules. Might confuse the olfactory circuits. I'm guessing the wolf has enhanced senses now.'

'You mean it *can* smell us.'

'Cyber-sniffers,' the Doctor agreed. 'There, that should do it.'

They set off down the tunnel again, but at a slightly more relaxed pace.

'How will we know if your agitation had any effect?' Olga wondered.

'Ask me that again in ten minutes.'

'How will that help?'

'If I'm still alive to answer, then we'll know it worked.'

Maybe it was wishful thinking, but the sound of the wolf did seem to be fading into the distance. After what Olga thought must be more than ten minutes, she began to relax a little. The tunnel was sloping uphill now, and after a few minutes more, they stopped to rest. Olga sank down on the cold stone floor.

'Is this a good time for you to explain to me what is happening?' she asked. She wasn't optimistic.

But the Doctor nodded thoughtfully. 'Cybership crashed ages back,' he said. 'We now know it was a colonisation ship or maybe a military transport. Whatever, it had a lot of Cybermen on board, mostly frozen to preserve them for the journey.'

'Like salting meat so it keeps through the winter?'

'Completely different, but yes – like salting meat. The point is they were going a long way. Think of the frozen Cybermen as the cargo. There was a crew as well, who obviously had to stay awake and with it to fly the ship.'

'The two that came after us?'

'More than two. There was another at the church, remember? Some of them were killed in the crash. If you can "kill" a Cyberman, given they're pretty much dead already. Worm and Drettle have been scavenging for bits and pieces from the crashed ship, though I don't think they ever went inside.'

'And they found Lord Ernhardt's hand? That is – the hand which the Watchman gave him.'

'Exactly. The Cybermen are programmed to survive, whatever the cost. So the crew have been scavenging from the graves – even adding to their occupants – to get hold of replacement limbs as they need them.'

Olga shuddered as she recalled the very human arm of one of the Cybermen. The woman's hand that had grabbed her by the ankle...

'Problem is,' the Doctor was saying, 'the organic material they scavenge isn't cybernetic. They just connect up the nervous system, so the limbs decay and need replacing.'

'What about the poisoning – the grey skin from the talisman jewellery?' Olga asked, as much to change the subject as anything.

'Unfortunate side effect. The reactor housing shattered, and fragments of the irradiated containment vessel got scattered across a field. People found them, thought they were interesting... Died.'

'And the wolves? What happened to them?'

'They're down on numbers, so the Cybermen adapted some of the wolves to act as extra guard dogs. Almost literally.'

'But if there are so many of these Cybermen, why didn't they simply awaken others from their "cargo"?'

'Not enough power. They've cannibalised what they can to set up a system that seeds the atmosphere and provokes lightning storms. Then they capture the energy from the lightning and store it. But without a power converter, and with just the one collection point at the church…'

'If there is just the one,' Olga pointed out. 'There is so much hidden beneath the surface of our village that I was not aware of before. They could have many of these…' She couldn't remember the word, and waved her hand to cover it. 'Things.'

The Doctor ignored her. 'It'll take centuries before they have anything like enough power to revive more Cybermen. It's probably taking most of what they collect just to keep the guards and the wolves going.'

'If you say so, Doctor.'

The Doctor jumped to his feet. 'Time to be moving.'

'Where are we going? Back to the church?'

'Up to the castle. I hope.' The Doctor turned to go, then turned quickly back to face Olga. He looked suddenly worried. 'You could be right. Didn't think of that.'

'What did you not think of?'

'That there might be multiple collection points for the lightning energy. They'd still need a converter, but it does potentially increase the efficiency of the system.'

'Which I assume is a bad thing.'

'Well, it's not good. Come on.'

They walked for what seemed like for ever. After the frenetic terror of escaping from Cybermen and

Cyber Wolves, the slow steady journey through the dark tunnels seemed almost boring.

After what seemed an age, the Doctor gave a cry of delight. He turned off the sonic screwdriver, and Olga saw that the tunnel ahead was illuminated by a pale flickering light.

'We're getting close,' the Doctor told her as they reached a burning sconce fixed to the wall. Olga could see another further along.

Along another tunnel, up a flight of crudely cut stone steps hewn from the rock floor, and down another tunnel... Olga was beginning to think of them more as passageways or corridors, probably just because of the fact they were lit. That they seemed 'lived in'.

Finally, they arrived at a heavy wooden door.

'This is it,' the Doctor announced. His eyes glittered with excitement in the guttering light. 'Can you tell where we are yet?'

'All the doors look alike to me, Doctor,' Olga confessed.

The Doctor pushed open the door and stood aside to let Olga go in first.

'Welcome back,' the Doctor said in a needlessly deep and doom-laden voice, 'to the lair of the Watchman.'

Chapter 9

The room was exactly as Olga remembered – the uneven stone floor; the vaulted ceiling; the table strewn with all manner of strange things; the curtained alcoves. And at the back of the room, holding a magnifying glass and looking up in surprise was the elderly, diminutive figure of the Watchman himself.

'What is the meaning of this?' he demanded as Olga entered the room. When the Doctor stepped into the room behind her, his surprise turned first to recognition, then to indignation and anger. 'You!'

'Oh,' the Doctor said, looking sheepish. 'Er, hi. Again. How's things?'

'How's things?' the Watchman echoed in astonishment. 'How's *things*?'

'Well, I was just asking.'

'Perhaps we should return later,' Olga said.

'You ransack my workshop,' the Watchman went on. 'You rummage through my collection of extremely rare and valuable objects. You help yourself to vital components.'

'We what?' Now the Doctor was indignant. 'What vital components?'

'Well, I don't know what they are exactly, but they must be important if you took them.'

'I didn't take anything,' the Doctor protested. 'Rummaged – yes, OK. Got me there. But no ransacking and certainly no helping myself.' He adjusted his bow tie and sniffed. 'I have enough vital and valuable components of my own, thank you very much.'

'I don't believe you,' the Watchman said. 'You were hiding under my table.'

'Might have been,' the Doctor confessed. 'But that's not a crime.'

'You hid under my table,' the Watchman went on. 'Then you ran off. And as soon as I was out of the way you came back and rummaged and ransacked and helped yourself. Look.' He strode over to the Doctor and caught his sleeve, dragging him round the workbench. He pointed at what, to Olga, looked like just another junk-strewn area of the table. 'Look!'

The Doctor frowned, and Olga guessed it meant nothing to him either.

'And not content with that, you even took parts of my latest experimentation subject.'

'Your what?'

'Here – look!'

The Watchman guided the Doctor across the room, Olga following close behind, to one of the alcoves. He let go of the Doctor's sleeve for long enough to pull back the curtain.

Olga realised what was behind the curtain just as the Watchman pulled it aside. She looked away. But she wasn't quick enough to avoid seeing Liza's mutilated body lying on an operating table in the alcove. There were incisions across the front of her body. And one arm was missing.

'I didn't do this,' the Doctor said.

'I thought you were a doctor.'

'I thought you mended watches.'

'That is immaterial.'

'Wait a minute,' the Doctor said. 'Olga – look at this.'

She still had her eyes shut. 'I am not looking at anything.'

'But we've seen an arm like that somewhere recently, remember?'

'I do not want to remember, thank you.'

But she did. She couldn't help remembering the slender, rotting female arm of the Cyberman…

'You didn't take her arm off?' the Doctor demanded.

'Of course not,' the Watchman said. 'What would I do with an *arm*? Are you trying to tell me it wasn't you?'

There was the sound of the curtain being drawn back across the alcove. 'I *am* telling you it wasn't me. You can open your eyes again now, Olga.'

The Doctor had moved on to another alcove now. He pulled back the curtain on this one, to reveal a stone plinth. A sheet was draped over the top. The Doctor grasped a corner of the sheet.

'No!' the Watchman warned.

But the Doctor ignored him. 'Time to find out what's really going on round here, don't you think?'

'And what is going on round here, as you put it, Doctor?'

The voice came from the doorway behind them. Olga and the Doctor both turned to see Lord and Lady Ernhardt standing just inside the room.

'That's what I want to know,' the Doctor said. 'But for one thing, the Watchman isn't quite as clever as he makes out.'

'I protest,' the Watchman said. 'This man has forced his way in here...'

'You want to see the source of the Watchman's knowledge?' the Doctor said loudly. 'You want to know where he gets his expertise? Oh, apart from the flotsam and jetsam that Worm and Drettle used to bring him I mean.'

The Watchman looked pale. 'What do you mean,

"used" to bring me?'

'They're dead,' the Doctor said simply.

'Dead?' the Watchman said in disbelief. 'But – they can't be dead. They were just here.'

'They were killed by your other friends.'

'What friends?' Lady Ernhardt asked.

'Friends like these!' the Doctor announced, and pulled the sheet away.

'Don't!' the Watchman exclaimed, hurrying across to stop the Doctor.

But he was too late.

Beneath the sheet, on top of the plinth, was a head. Rusted, dented, tarnished, with one of the side struts cracked and out of alignment, it was the head of a Cyberman.

And it was screaming. As soon as the sheet came off, the head let out an unearthly screech. If Cybermen ever felt pain, this was surely what it sounded like.

'Put the sheet back – quickly!' the Watchman urged. 'It can't bear the light. For pity's sake!'

'Doctor!' Lord Ernhardt urged.

But like Olga, the Doctor was staring in horror at the Cyberman's eyes. Or rather, at the sockets where the eyes had been. There was a pinpoint of light in the centre of each, but the edges of each eye socket had been torn open. Rivets surrounded each eye, hammered clumsily into place. Oil stains surrounded the eyes, running down the face like tears.

The Doctor flung the sheet back over the head, and immediately the screeching stopped.

The Cyberhead's words were forced out, disjointed, scrapings of sound: 'My... eyes. No light... my eyes...'

The Watchman hurried to adjust the sheet. 'I have done what I can for him. I tried to repair the eyes. But still – the pain caused by light...' He glared at the Doctor.

'But – what is it?' Lady Ernhardt gasped.

'A relic. I call it the Oracle. And yes, the Doctor is right, it has helped guide my work. It has helped me in my efforts to save your son.'

'It's a Plague Warrior – a *Cyberman*,' Olga said.

'Or what's left of one,' the Doctor added. 'Guiding you, yes, but to its own ends.'

'I think perhaps you should explain yourself, Doctor,' Lord Ernhardt said.

The Watchman opened his mouth to object, but Lord Ernhardt silenced him with a look. 'I think we'd all like to hear what the Doctor has to tell us.'

With help from Olga, the Doctor gave a quick explanation of the plague and of the Cybermen and their crashed ship. Lord and Lady Ernhardt listened in near silence, and the Watchman too seemed genuinely interested to learn more about the strange components and mechanisms he had discovered.

Finally the Doctor came to the end of his story. 'We should be able to seal them down there. We can cave in the tunnels, disconnect their equipment in the church tower, and just let them power down.'

'Like going to sleep?' Lady Ernhardt asked.

'I suppose,' the Doctor agreed. He walked slowly round the Watchman's table. 'I imagine the "Oracle" here has been slowly gathering the components it needs to get the Watchman to build a functioning power converter. Luckily, all the necessary components are right here on this...' He stopped.

'What is it, Doctor?' Olga asked.

'What have you done with the main power converter assembly?' the Doctor demanded. He stared across at the Watchman. 'Yes, I'm talking to you.'

'I've done nothing with anything,' the little man protested. 'I told you – when you barged in here just now, I told you.' He turned to Olga. 'Didn't I tell him?'

'He did tell you,' she agreed.

'Tell me what?'

'That someone has removed some of my equipment, my mechanisms.'

'He thought you had taken it,' Olga reminded him.

'Why would I want it?'

'Why would anyone?' Lord Ernhardt asked.

'Well, obviously because it can convert the lightning from the storms and provide the Cybermen with the power they need to...' The Doctor took a deep breath and turned round on the spot. 'Oh no.'

'But there are no Cybermen up *here*,' Olga pointed out. Even as she said it, she felt a sudden chill of fear. 'Are there?'

As if in answer, there was a crash of metal from the far side of the room. Components and debris were piled up in one of the alcoves. There was no curtain, just a heap of metal and plastic. Olga watched in horror as the whole pile shifted. Nuts and bolts, rods and cables rolled down and across the floor as something forced its way out of the centre of the heap.

The unmistakable head of a Cyberman – undamaged and intact – thrust up through the sea of mechanisms as the creature pushed itself upright. As it stood, Olga saw with horror that one of its legs was human. The tattered remains of Stefan the gravedigger's trousers clung to the thigh.

In its hand, the Cyberman clutched an oblong metal box which Olga was sure must be the vital equipment the Doctor had described. It held it aloft like a trophy.

'We will revive,' the Cyberman grated.

Chapter 10

The Watchman stepped forward, fascinated. 'A complete automaton! Up until now I have only seen the components, the pieces.'

He turned to the Doctor.

'How does it work?'

'Never mind how it works!' The Doctor grabbed the man and pulled him back, away from the Cyberman.

'What is it?' Lord Ernhardt demanded. He put his arm protectively round his wife. 'What have you brought here, Watchman?'

The Watchman shook his head nervously. 'Not me.'

'It's a Cyberman,' the Doctor told them. 'And we need to keep well clear of it.'

The Cyberman watched, unmoving and impassive. Like a statue.

'Is that the power converter you spoke of?' Lady Ernhardt asked, pointing to the device the Cyberman held.

The Doctor nodded. 'We have to dismantle it. It works by induction, so it doesn't need a direct connection. It'll be gathering and converting power already, probably storing it up in its internal batteries ready to be plugged into the Cyber systems. And if that happens...' He left the thought unfinished.

'We will revive,' the Cyberman said again – as if it was a challenge. It took a step forward, and the Doctor pulled the Watchman back another pace.

'I'm afraid I don't understand any of this,' Lord Ernhardt said. 'Except that this... *creature* is somehow a threat to us?'

'And then some,' the Doctor agreed.

'This one and others,' Olga added.

'And if we don't get that power converter off him this place will be overrun with Cyber-Plague Warriors before you can sneeze,' the Doctor said.

Lord Ernhardt stepped towards the Cyberman. Lady Ernhardt put her hand on his arm, but he carefully removed it, patted her shoulder and smiled reassuringly, before taking another step forward.

'Then you had better put that device down, hadn't you,' he said to the Cyberman.

The Cyberman turned its head slightly, angling it

to look down at the man. It did not reply.

'Put it down, sir!' Ernhardt's voice was loud but calm and full of authority.

'Um,' the Doctor said. 'I really don't think…'

But Ernhardt was striding across the room, eyes fixed on the Cyberman. 'I am the authority in this area, I'll have you know. I am the law. And I order you to lay down that device or suffer the consequences.'

'Shall I fetch the guards?' the Watchman asked. His voice was strung out and taut with fear.

'No time,' Lord Ernhardt said, without turning from the Cyberman. 'And no need.'

'Alexander,' his wife said quietly. 'Let me…'

'I can handle this, my dear.'

'Doctor!' Olga hissed. 'You have to stop this. It will kill him.'

'You think you are invincible,' Lord Ernhardt was saying, 'because you wear armour. But I tell you, my friend, things are not always what they seem.'

'Friend?' the Cyberman countered.

'If you put that device down and discuss terms, then yes – potentially, friend.'

'Ernhardt!' the Doctor warned.

'Cybermen do not discuss terms. Cybermen are not friends.'

'Enemy, then,' Ernhardt said simply. And launched himself at the Cyberman.

Olga screamed. Lady Ernhardt's hands were over

her mouth. The Doctor gave a cry of warning and the Watchman whimpered.

The Cyberman raised its arm – the same almost casual gesture that Olga had seen kill Drettle. This time, however, the effect was different. The Cyberman's blow connected with Lord Ernhardt's gloved hand. Metal clanged on metal as the blow was parried.

But the force of it still sent Lord Ernhardt stumbling backwards. He sprawled across the table, knocking equipment and components flying. As he straightened up, he pulled a long metal bar from amongst the detritus. It rang against the wooden table like a sword being drawn from its scabbard as Lord Ernhardt turned to face the Cyberman again.

The metal figure stepped forward. The power converter hung from one hand. The other was raised to deliver another blow. But before it could strike, Ernhardt slammed the long metal bar into the side of the Cyberman's head. The room echoed with the sound of the blow. Sparks spat from the point of impact. The Cyberman reeled away.

Quick as lightning, the Doctor dashed forward and grabbed the power converter, ripping it from the Cyberman's grasp. The creature turned towards him – and the metal bar crashed into its back, knocking it forwards. The Cyberman collapsed to its knees. It amazed Olga that Lord Ernhardt could deliver his blows with such force – he was a slight man, and didn't look that strong. Then she remembered how the stone wall had shattered under the blow from his metal hand. Perhaps the Cyberman had indeed met its match.

Ernhardt stepped towards his opponent, the bar raised above his head. The Cyberman was faster than it looked, lashing out in a sweeping arc with one arm. It knocked Ernhardt sideways and he collapsed with a groan, the air forced from his lungs.

His wife made to go and help, but the Doctor put his arm out to stop her.

'His leg!' Olga shouted. She remembered the way the Doctor had stopped the Cyberman that had grabbed her. 'He has a real leg, not metal.'

Ernhardt nodded his thanks as he staggered back to his feet. The Cyberman was almost on him. From the ground, Ernhardt jabbed with the bar. He stabbed, as if it was a sword, right into the Cyberman's human leg. There was a loud crack as the metal connected with bone. The knee gave way beneath the creature's weight and it sank down on one side before falling headlong.

'Sorry, Stefan,' Olga gasped. Immediately she wondered why she was so upset – it wasn't as if the leg had anything to do with Stefan any more.

Getting back to his feet, Ernhardt stepped up to where the Cyberman was struggling to stand. The human leg gave way again. The metal creature looked up at Ernhardt standing over it, bar raised like an executioner axe, gripped tight in the man's gloved hand.

Olga watched in horrified fascination as the bar swept down. It hammered into the Cyberman's head at the point where the neck connected. The head was knocked sideways in a shower of sparks. Wires and tubes spilled out from its broken neck, the head still attached but leaning drunkenly to the side.

A second, harder blow sent the head flying across the room. It smashed into the wall and fell battered, dented and inert to the floor. The Cyberman's kneeling body continued to sway, arms moving spasmodically, flames licking up from the hole in its shattered neck.

The Doctor pulled Ernhardt away. 'Down – everyone get down!' he shouted.

They ducked down behind the table, just as the remains of the Cyberman exploded. Olga shrieked as something hot caught in her hair. The Doctor leaned across and brushed it aside. Burning metal fragments were raining down on them.

Then, abruptly, everything was quiet and still.

'Is it over?' the Watchman asked, his voice trembling.

'Over?' the Doctor stared at him. 'It's barely begun.' He thrust the power converter towards the man. 'Here, give me a hand dismantling this. Shouldn't be beyond your capabilities.'

The Watchman bristled, about to protest.

'Just do it,' Lady Ernhardt snapped.

'Can't you simply smash it to pieces?' Lord Ernhardt asked. He was sweating and breathless from the fight. Blood ran in a thin trickle from a cut just under his eye.

'Dangerous,' the Doctor told him. 'If this thing's stored up power from the storms, then we could release that in one big eurgh of lightning right here in this room. In which case – pow! "Eurgh" and "pow" are technical terms,' he added. 'No, got to dismantle it very carefully.'

As he spoke he handed one end of the converter to the Watchman. 'Here, hold this tight.'

The Doctor then twisted his end of the converter. The casing broke away to reveal a mass of dials and gauges and wires and tubes packed inside.

'Now what?' the Watchman asked.

The Doctor was staring at the dials. 'Now we have good news and bad news.'

But before the Doctor could elaborate, Lord Ernhardt let out a cry. It was a mixture of surprise, pain, and fear. His gloved hand was raised, fingers clenching in the air.

'What is it?' his wife immediately asked, concerned. 'My love – what's wrong?'

'My hand,' he gasped. 'I can't – it's… Help me!'

His whole hand was shaking. With his other hand he grasped his own wrist.

'Cybernetic hand,' the Doctor realised. 'Even

with the innards replaced they can still control it.'

As he spoke, the hand broke free of Ernhardt's grip, lashing out at the power converter the Doctor held. Ernhardt was pulled after it, his face a mask of pain and anger.

The Doctor ducked out of the way, and the gloved fingers closed on empty air. He gave the power converter to the Watchman and grabbed Ernhardt's gloved hand with both his, holding it tight.

'What is it doing?' Olga gasped.

'Trying to get the power converter. It'll turn it back on.'

Ernhardt was on his feet, pulled towards the Watchman by his clenching hand. He and the Doctor seemed joined in a strange wrestling match as they tried to pull his hand back.

'But how does it know?' the Watchman said. 'Hands can't *see*!'

'Who cares?' the Doctor said. 'Maybe it's making use of the host's nervous system and sensory capacity, I don't know. Just give us a...' His voiced tailed off as he realised what he was about to say. '... A hand.'

But the word was almost lost as Lord Ernhardt seemed to throw the Doctor off him – sending his gangly figure cartwheeling away across the room.

Ernhardt gave a cry of pain and fear as he lunged at the Watchman. The little man could do nothing as the gloved hand closed on his throat.

Olga ran to help, clawing at the glove with her own hands, trying to dig her nails into the unyielding metal beneath the glove. But with no effect.

The Watchman's spectacles slipped from his face and fell to the floor. A moment later, his body was hurtling through the air after the Doctor. But whereas the Doctor had slumped groggily to the floor, the Watchman hit the wall head first. There was a crunch of breaking bone, and he sagged to the ground, his head lolling at an awkward angle, his eyes glazed and unseeing.

A gloved hand reached down towards the fallen power converter. Shrugged off, Olga fell to the floor beside the vital piece of equipment. She grabbed for it, but too late. Despite his efforts, Lord Ernhardt's hand snatched it up.

The Doctor had recovered and hurried to the Watchman. But it was obvious the poor man was dead. Sadly, the Doctor closed the man's eyes before turning to face Ernhardt, his own eyes burning with anger.

'I should have listened to him,' the Doctor said. 'How can it see – what a good question.'

'Doctor…' Ernhardt spluttered. 'Doctor – I can't…'

'You have to fight it!'

The Doctor rushed back across the room. Olga was dragging herself back to her feet. But what could she do?

'The head – the Cyberman's head,' the Doctor told her. 'It must be directing the hand's movements. That's how it can see. They're linked, both part of the Cyber network.'

Olga sort of understood. There was a connection between the hand and the head that had come off the Cyberman before it exploded. The metal head looked cold and inert, staring like a skull in the catacombs across the room through dark, blank eyes.

She glanced at the discarded metal rod Lord Ernhardt had used to attack the Cyberman. But she knew she couldn't destroy the head, so she didn't try. Olga pulled an oily cloth from under a pile of wires and metal fragments on the table and threw it over the severed head.

At once, Lord Ernhardt's hand stopped fighting against him. He breathed a sigh of relief, and pulled the power converter from its grasp with his other hand. But the respite was brief. At once, the hand was alive again, snatching blindly for the power converter. Failing to find it, the hand aimed instead for Lord Ernhardt's throat. He gave a startled cry of panic and fear as the hand came at him.

Then another hand grabbed the gloved fist, holding it tight and dragging it away. A second hand closed round them both. Lady Ernhardt's face was an expressionless mask as she pulled her husband's possessed hand away from his throat.

The Doctor reached across to help. But he didn't

need to. Already Lady Ernhardt had the gloved hand under control, holding it fast. Then with a sudden, violent movement, she wrenched the hand backwards. It disconnected from Lord Ernhardt's wrist. He fell away as a shower of sparks exploded from the end of the gloved hand. Lady Ernhardt held the hand for a moment, then hurled it to the floor.

The hand scrabbled on the stone slabs, crawling hesitantly forwards. Olga snatched up the metal rod. It was heavy, but with a strength enhanced by fear and adrenalin she raised it above her head before smashing it down on the hand writhing on the floor. Again and again she hammered at it, until the thing lay broken, smoking, and still.

She dropped the rod and it clattered to the floor beside the hand.

The four of them stood breathless from the exertion.

'How did you do that?' the Doctor asked at last. He was talking to Lady Ernhardt.

She met his gaze. 'It was attacking my husband.'

'No, I meant…' The Doctor sighed. 'Never mind.' He returned his attention to the power converter.

'You said…' Lord Ernhardt hesitated as he caught his breath. 'You said that there was a problem?'

'Before I was so rudely interrupted,' the Doctor agreed. 'Good news and bad news.'

'And what is this news?' Olga asked.

'Well, the good news is that we can just destroy

this power converter and make sure that the Cybermen don't get any more energy from it.'

'Any *more*?' Olga said.

'Yes, well that's the bad news. I thought it was a battery that stored the power up until it was wired in to where it's needed.'

'And it isn't?' She didn't understand what he was saying, but the Doctor's expression was grave.

'Sadly not. It passes the power straight on – through induction, same way as it gathers the power in the first place. There's no way of knowing how long it's been working, how much power it processed, or where it sent it.'

He bent down to place the power converter carefully on the floor. Inspecting his work, he then moved it slightly so it aligned neatly with the edges of the nearest flagstones. He reached out and picked up the metal rod that Olga had dropped.

Then the Doctor straightened up, raised the rod, and smashed it down hard on the power converter. The metal component exploded, making Olga jump back in surprise. The Doctor didn't so much as flinch. Instead, he hit it again.

'And once for luck,' he said, hitting it a third time. But the converter was obviously broken – pieces had bent or broken off and the inside was a charred mess.

'This power the Cybermen somehow acquired?' Lord Ernhardt asked, nursing the broken stump of his wrist.

The Doctor turned to face him. 'You want to know where the power went? What they used it for?'

'I think we all do,' Lady Ernhardt said. Olga nodded her agreement.

'Absolutely,' the Doctor agreed. 'And you can just bet it's nothing good.'

Chapter 11

The walk back to the village was every bit as wet and stormy as when they had walked up. It seemed so long ago – so much had happened. Olga struggled to keep up with the Doctor as he strode along the downward-sloping path from the castle. It was slippery and hazardous, the water from the constant rain running off and leaving it slick with mud.

Caplan and three guards were with them. They seemed to have no trouble keeping up, and no interest in how Olga was faring. She was determined not to ask them to slow down, though she was sure the Doctor would as soon as he realised there was a problem.

Lightning forked across the sky. Olga tried to imagine how much raw power was in each streak of fire, how much energy the Plague Warriors – the *Cybermen* – had somehow extracted from the sky. And what had they used it for? The Doctor offered no thoughts on the subject other than a sudden announcement that he was returning to the village.

As the path evened out, Olga hurried to catch up with the Doctor.

'Ah, there you are,' he said, without looking.

'Here I am,' she agreed. 'But where are we going? I mean, I know we're going to the village, but why do we need the guards? What are you intending?'

'I'm intending to stop this,' he said. 'Too many people have died.'

'You mean the plague – the poisoning?'

'And Worm and Drettle and the Watchman. Stefan the gravedigger too – he didn't die of radiation poisoning.'

'And how will you stop it?'

'With your help.' He turned to look at her, grinning. But the amusement didn't touch his eyes which remained grey and cold. 'And Caplan and his colleagues here. That's a point,' he went on, raising his voice so the guard commander could hear him over the rain. 'Why does Lord Ernhardt need guards at all? It's not like you've been at war.'

'From what you say, Doctor, we are at war now,' Caplan growled back.

'Fair point. And well made. But up until I arrived…' He paused to mutter 'Story of my life,' so quietly only Olga heard him. 'But up until now, you haven't been at war, have you?'

Caplan shrugged. 'It's a sign of status, having private guards. Most of us have other duties as well as guarding the castle gates. Kris here works in the kitchen.'

One of the other guards nodded and smiled – showing off blackened and broken teeth.

'Sounds healthy,' the Doctor said.

'And you never know when the marshals will call a muster,' Caplan went on. 'Each lord has a duty to provide troops in time of crisis.'

'It doesn't have to be a war,' Olga told the Doctor. 'The last crisis was a landslide. The marshals called a muster to dig out survivors and rebuild the town.'

The Doctor nodded. 'Very altruistic. So we could ask these marshals to muster up some troops to help us if we need them?'

'We're a bit out of the way here,' Caplan pointed out.

'It would take two days to get a message to the nearest marshal in Malkeburg,' Olga said.

'Another two days to send out the muster,' Caplan added. 'Perhaps a week before help arrived. If we were lucky.'

'You need email,' the Doctor told them. 'Or at least the telephone.'

'Probably,' Olga agreed, though she had no idea what he meant.

'Who'd want to help us anyway?' the guard with broken teeth asked sullenly.

'You'd be surprised,' the Doctor told him. 'Now come on, no time to waste. Last one back to the tavern's buying the crisps.'

And to Olga's horror, he broke into a run.

By the time Olga got to the tavern, she was drenched. The Doctor was standing at the bar with the three guards talking to what seemed like most of the adult villagers.

Klaus saw Olga arrive, and his stern expression faded into a smile. He pushed through the other villagers, and ushered Olga towards the fire so she could warm up and dry out.

'What's going on?' she asked quietly, struggling to keep her teeth from chattering. 'What's he been saying?'

'That he wants our help,' Klaus whispered back. 'He's very persuasive.'

'Yes,' Olga agreed. That was certainly true. 'What are you grinning at?' she asked as Klaus continued to smile at her. It was becoming a little unsettling.

'Nothing,' he said.

But he kept on smiling. Olga realised that she was smiling back.

Their smiles faded though as the Doctor's voice reached them: '... which is why my good friend Klaus over there will be showing you the way while

Olga and I take the lead...'

If Caplan was offended that the Doctor put Klaus in charge of organising the villagers, he didn't show it. Klaus himself would far rather have had Caplan in charge – he probably knew what he was doing, for one thing. And for another, he wasn't likely to be as scared as Klaus.

The Doctor had drawn a quick and rough sketch of the catacomb tunnels on a flimsy piece of paper he unfolded from his pocket. He showed it to Caplan, Klaus, Olga and Old Nicolai.

'Napkin from the *Titanic*,' he told them. 'Hopefully it's dried out a bit by now.' Then he produced a stub of pencil and explained what he expected Klaus and the others to do.

'So we will be a diversionary attack,' Caplan said.

'Well, "attack" is a bit strong, and it won't be much of a diversion, but yes – spot on. Exactly right.'

'We keep the Plague Warriors occupied while you and Olga...' Klaus hesitated. That was as much as he actually understood. 'While you and Olga, er, do something else.'

'Spot on again. Top of the class, Klaus. So – everyone clear on what we're doing?'

There was a general shaking of heads. Old Nicolai muttered that no it wasn't at all clear.

'Good,' the Doctor announced. 'Well, let's be getting on with it, then.'

This prompted more muttering and head-shaking until the Doctor seemed to get the message, sighed, and tried again.

Ten minutes later, Klaus found himself addressing a group of the fittest and more able-bodied village men. The group included Old Nicolai, who insisted on joining them.

'The Doctor and Olga are going to find the lair of the Plague Warriors and…' Well Klaus wasn't quite sure about that. 'And sort them out once and for all,' he decided.

There was some cheering at this. But one voice called out: 'Why them? A stranger and a schoolteacher.'

'When we don't even have a school,' another of the villagers added.

Klaus drew himself up to his full and not-inconsiderable height. 'Can you think of anyone better?' he demanded. 'The Doctor's the only one here who understands any of this. And a schoolteacher who can teach when there's no school is someone to be proud of, not to jeer at, Henri.'

'Sorry, Klaus,' Henri conceded. 'We all know that you and Olga…' He shrugged.

'Me and Olga what?' Klaus was angry and confused now. 'What are you talking about?'

'Nothing. It doesn't matter.'

'No – I'd like to know.'

'Klaus,' Old Nicolai said gently, 'if you don't

154

know already, then you never will.'

Klaus frowned at the grizzled old man, but he refused to elaborate. Just grinned. In fact, now Klaus looked, everyone seemed to be grinning. Well, that was a good thing, he decided given what he had to ask them to do.

'Olga and the Doctor are going to the Plague Warriors' lair,' he repeated. 'It's up to us to keep the Plague Warriors – the ones who are awake – up to us to keep them busy while the Doctor does… whatever it is that the Doctor is going to do. Is that clear?'

'As it'll ever be,' Old Nicolai said. 'Let's get on with it. We'll need torches. Firebrands. And anything we can use as a weapon.'

Klaus nodded. 'Spades, axes, pitchforks, staves – anything. Collect what you can and we'll meet as soon as we can be ready.'

'Where do we meet?' one of them asked.

Klaus shivered as he said it: 'The churchyard. Beside poor Liza's empty grave.'

In the event, it was the Doctor and Olga who descended into the dark maw of the grave. The Doctor sent Klaus, Caplan, Old Nicolai and the others to get into the catacombs from the crypt under the church.

'And check the tower first, just in case there's one of them hiding up there. Make a lot of noise as you go into the catacombs – with a bit of luck, that should draw the Cybermen towards you to see what's going on and counter any threat.'

'The threat being us, I take it,' Caplan said. He hefted his sword, testing its weight.

'Absolutely. You need to make the Cybermen think you're a major threat to their survival.' The Doctor looked round at the group of villagers with their pitchforks, shovels, burning firebrands and – in one case – a broken sickle. 'Work on that.'

The Doctor jumped down into the grave, reached back up to help Olga as Klaus lowered her after him.

'Oh,' the Doctor added as he ducked his head down towards the broken floor of the grave. 'And watch out for the wolves.'

Klaus's voice reached the Doctor and Olga as they lowered themselves into the tunnel below: 'What? What wolves?'

Once again, the Doctor's sonic screwdriver lit their way. And once again, Olga did her best to avoid looking at the pale skeletal remains that littered the passageways or stared out from shelves. Just as before, she failed. But somehow it seemed less unsettling now. Perhaps she was getting used to it, but that in itself was worrying. She didn't want ever to take death for granted – because that implied she was taking life for granted too.

They made their way slowly, carefully, and quietly through the catacombs, listening for any hint of Cybermen or for the sounds that might suggest

Klaus and the others had started their 'distraction'. Olga was acutely aware that the distraction could – and probably would – result in more injury and even death. Something else not to think about. She couldn't bear it if Klaus…

'Why did you bring me?' she whispered close behind the Doctor's ear.

He gave no indication that he had heard her, but she was sure he had.

'What do you need me for?' she hissed.

'I like company,' he whispered back. 'Maybe it's the intellectual conversation.'

'You like being alone,' she told him. 'I can see it in your eyes, I can hear it in your voice as you try to be patient with us when we don't immediately understand what you mean.'

'Perhaps it's good for me. Patience is a virtue.'

So he wasn't denying it, Olga realised. She bit her lip as she summoned the courage to ask him what she really wanted to know. 'Have you brought me with you to be another distraction?'

'A what?' He stopped and turned, and looked her in the eye.

'A distraction,' she repeated. 'Like Klaus and Caplan and the others. Someone for the Plague Warriors to kill while you do… whatever you have to do.'

'Oh no.' He seemed genuinely surprised. 'No, no, no, not ever. Never. No. Did you think that?'

'Then why?'

'I told you – I enjoy your company.'

'No one enjoys my company. I make the children learn when they want to go out and play, and I remind the adults of how little they know.'

The Doctor sighed. 'Tell me about it,' he murmured. Then, louder: 'You are not a distraction, and I think more people crave your company than you realise.'

'And I am here because?'

The Doctor brandished his sonic screwdriver, waving it in front of her eyes. 'Because when I disconnect the power systems, I'll need to concentrate. It's a difficult and fiddly job which will take a bit of time. And I'll need someone to hold the light, all right?'

Which actually made sense. She was relieved, even if that was all he needed her for. 'All right,' she said.

'Good. Er – I wasn't too impatient and arrogant there, was I?'

'No Doctor.'

His face crinkled into a huge grin as he turned away. 'Liar.'

The crypt was lit only by the smoky, guttering light from the firebrands held by some of the villagers. Klaus led the way, grateful for Caplan beside him.

'How do you get through something like this?'

Klaus asked quietly.

'Lord knows,' Caplan told him. 'I think of my wife and my daughter, I suppose. Promise myself that I'll see them again.'

Klaus nodded. He didn't have a family, so instead he thought of Olga, and found that helped dispel the fear for his own safety. But now he was worrying about her.

They made their way through the crypt and into the catacombs. Klaus had never been down here before – had never even known it existed. From the reactions of the others, neither had anyone else. Only Old Nicolai nodded and smiled grimly as if this was exactly what he had expected.

Klaus checked the map the Doctor had sketched, and led them along what he hoped was the right passageway. A rat appeared from beneath a shattered skeleton at the side of the tunnel and scampered on ahead of them, soon lost again in shadows.

The passage led to a junction with several others. With Caplan's help, Klaus worked out which path to take, and they continued on their way. Just as the Doctor had described, the tunnel led to a huge cavern with other tunnels leading off. As he'd told them, there was a metal wall on the far side of the cavern, with a large hole ripped in it. Debris was strewn across the ground, spilling out of the hole in the side of the strange ship the Plague Warriors had sailed here all those years ago.

And sprawled across the debris was the shattered body of Drettle. Of Worm's corpse there was no sign.

'So what do we do now?' Kris asked nervously.

'We make a noise,' Klaus told him. 'Just like the Doctor said. Bring the Plague Warriors out of their strange ship to see what's happening.'

'And we should take Drettle's body back,' Old Nicolai said. 'Bury him properly.'

'Let's hope he's the only one,' Caplan muttered.

The simple process of moving Drettle's body was noisy enough. He was a big man, and it took three of them to carry him down from where he had fallen. The heap of scrap and rubbish shifted noisily under their feet. Metal clanked on metal. They carried Drettle to the entrance of the passageway they had entered by and laid him respectfully on the ground.

When Klaus turned from closing the dead man's eyes, he saw the Plague Warriors. Two of them stood in the gaping hole in the metal wall. They stared back at him through blank, dead eyes across the cavern. Then, slowly but deliberately, with measured movements, they stepped out onto the pile of debris.

One of the metal men had a human arm. The other was dented and scorched, but with what looked like discoloured, rotting flesh grafted across its chest.

'We're a distraction,' Caplan murmured so that only Klaus could hear. 'We don't have to fight them if we can avoid it. Just keep them here so the Doctor can do his work.'

Klaus nodded, picking up the shovel he'd put down so he could help carry Drettle. 'We came to recover our friend's body,' he announced. He could hear as well as feel the tremor in his own voice.

The Plague Warriors continued their slow advance. Klaus gripped the handle of his shovel tighter.

One of the Plague Warriors raised its human arm, pointing across at Klaus and the others. Its voice was a metallic rasp, like a rusty bolt being drawn back.

'You belong to us. You shall be like us.'

The Doctor led the way to the same tunnel as before. Again, Olga followed him through the hole in the metal skin of the ship and into the blood-red interior.

Finger to his lips, the Doctor beckoned for Olga to follow. Their progress was quicker this time as they knew the way.

At first they proceeded cautiously. But soon after they were inside, they heard shouts echoing along the metal corridors. The clash of metal on metal. A sound like sudden thunder which made the Doctor frown.

'Energy discharge. Hope they're all right.'

Olga hoped so too, but she didn't trust herself to speak. She just followed the Doctor deeper and deeper into the ship, hoping against hope that Klaus – and the others of course, but mainly Klaus – would be all right.

Finally, they reached the gantries, and navigated their way round the area where the floor had dropped away. There was a pale glow from the vast chamber where they had found the sleeping Cybermen. Mist hung low over the floor like it did in the graveyard on an autumn morning.

'Now comes the tricky bit,' the Doctor said quietly. He brandished his sonic screwdriver. 'Don't want to turn the lights on – that didn't go so well last time. So this is your big moment.'

Olga was looking round. Her eyes had adjusted to the misty gloom, but even so... 'I don't think you'll need the light, Doctor.'

'How do you mean? Oh.' His expression froze. It should have been comical, but instead Olga found it worrying.

The light around them was definitely increasing. The mist was more visible now, cascading off the wall like a waterfall. There was a low hum, building in volume. Then the impossible pitter-patter of rain.

'What's happening?' Olga asked. She could see her breath as she spoke, but even so, she realised: 'It's getting warmer.'

'They're channelling the power into the hibernation cells.'

The Doctor took hold of Olga's shoulders, moving her back from the vast wall of sleeping figures. It was clearly visible now as the lights came up.

'We need somewhere to hide.' The Doctor let go

of her shoulders, took her hand instead, and pulled Olga after him to a large metal box jutting out from the side wall. The surface of it was covered with levers and buttons, dials and gauges.

'But – aren't you going to stop them? Cut off the power?'

The Doctor shook his head. 'Too late for that. They're using the power already.'

'For the lights?'

'And the temperature. After all these years they finally have enough power to wake the other Cybermen.' His face was deathly pale. 'I'm sorry Olga – but we're too late.'

Chapter 12

The lights continued to brighten. The faint pattering of falling water became steadier and more insistent. The mist rolling off the wall thinned so that the Doctor and Olga could see the front of the hibernation cells. It looked like a giant honeycomb, each cell tessellated with the next in a vast array.

At first, Olga could see nothing through the fading mist. Then she made out the water dripping from the membranes that covered the cells. Beneath, embossed on each cell, was a symbol – a stylised head of a Cyberman, black against the translucent sheen of the covering. The water running from the symbols made it look like the faces were crying.

Inside each of the cells, a darker patch became distinct within the light. Moving – unfolding. Like a child curled up into a ball slowly uncurling and flexing its muscles. Except these were too large to be children – giants, like the Plague Warrior Cybermen Olga had already seen.

As she watched in horrified fascination, the first of the Cybermen began to break out of its cell. A fist punched through the membrane, silver fingers in a tight fist, then opening like a flower sensing the sun. The metal arm thrust after it, tearing through the material, ripping downwards to make a gap large enough for the Cyberman's head. The creature's shoulders ripped aside what was left of the membrane as the Cyberman stepped out through the shredded material.

It emerged onto a narrow walkway outside the cell. For a moment the blank skull-metal face seemed to stare directly at Olga. Then the figure straightened up.

Above, below and beside it, other Cybermen mirrored the first in out-of-step, time-lapsed movements. Olga could not count how many there were. The whole wall of cells was writhing with metallic life. Fists – arms – heads – Cybermen forcing their way out of their icy tomb and moving inexorably to the huge ladders cut into the wall at either side. A vast army descending to the floor of the chamber…

'You know,' the Doctor said quietly to Olga, 'this is exactly the sort of thing I was hoping to avoid.'

'What do we do now?' she whispered back.

'Well...' He tapped his sonic screwdriver against his front teeth as he considered. 'I've found that in these sorts of situations the best thing, usually, is to make a run for it.'

Olga was horrified. 'But they'll see us as soon as we move.'

'If we don't move they'll see us soon enough anyway. That's the danger with the run-for-it plan, though – there's always a chance you'll get caught and killed.'

'Does that ever happen?'

'Been caught lots of times,' the Doctor admitted. 'Killed? Well, not so often. You coming?' He grabbed Olga's hand and leaped to his feet.

'Once would be enough for me,' she said. 'More than enough.'

But he probably didn't hear her as they raced for the steps up to the gantry. Olga did not dare to look back until she got there. Then she risked a glance over her shoulder.

As she had feared, the Cybermen were coming after them. But the silver giants seemed sluggish – as if they hadn't properly woken up yet.

'Power levels still a bit low,' the Doctor told her. 'Every cloud has a silver lining. Come on.'

It was a repeat of the nightmare journey Olga had made with the Doctor earlier. Except that this time it was the sounds from ahead that spurred her on rather than the threat behind. They could hear the sounds of the battle outside the ship. What was happening – were Klaus and the others all right? Olga was desperate to know.

'We have to help them,' she gasped as she ran.

'We have to warn them,' the Doctor said.

'Warn them?'

'There are a hundred hairy Cybermen coming after us, probably heading for Klaus and the others. Well,' he clarified, 'not a hundred exactly. And not hairy as such. But lots, and nasty.'

Not surprisingly, Caplan and his two guards made the most impact. They hacked and jabbed with their swords at the advancing Plague Warriors. The other villagers thrust burning torches at them, or tried to get in close enough to use a shovel or axe.

Kris was wounded – his arm burned by a bolt of lightning that shot from one of the Plague Warriors' arms. As soon as it fired, before the creature could lower its metal arm, Caplan stepped forward and thrust his sword into the tube that had spat fire across the cavern. He twisted the blade, and there was no more lightning, so his efforts had an effect.

But even so, the Plague Warriors showed inhuman strength and determination. They advanced step by step, parrying swords and shovels with their arms. The human arm of one of them was shredded. But the creature showed no pain or anxiety.

A blow from one Plague Warrior sent Old Nicolai sprawling backwards. Klaus caught him, and saw the fear and confusion in the old man's eyes.

'You and Kris take Drettle's body and get back to the village,' Klaus told him.

It was a measure of how serious the situation was that Nicolai did not argue. Instead, he staggered over to where Kris sat with his back to the rock wall, nursing his wounded arm and looking pale as death.

Caplan was also backing away, motioning for his guards and the other villagers to follow.

'They're coming after us,' he said to Klaus. 'That's good.'

'Good?'

'Keeps them away from the Doctor and the schoolteacher.'

He was right – it was good for Olga. Not so good for Klaus and the villagers who had to defend themselves every step of the way. Turn and run, and the Plague Warriors would be on them in an instant. There seemed to be no way to stop them. But they were holding their own – the villagers had taken on the Plague Warriors and they were still alive.

'So what's the plan?' Caplan asked.

'You're asking me?' Klaus was surprised.

The big guard commander paused to slice a blow across the closest Plague Warrior's chest. It tore into the flesh grafted into the metal, and the creature staggered back a pace.

'You're in charge,' Caplan said.

'Doesn't mean I know what I'm doing.' He thrust his shovel forwards, butting the other Plague Warrior with a clang of metal on metal.

'Often the way,' Caplan said with a wry smile.

'What would you suggest?'

'Retreat, carefully. As far as the church.'

'And then?'

'Try to shut these creatures out. Barricade the crypt door. Might give us time to get back to the village.'

It was as good a plan as any. Better than anything Klaus had thought of. So he nodded his agreement. Then he heard the sound from behind them.

'Ah,' Caplan said, his smile fading as he too heard the noise, echoing along the tunnel. 'We were forgetting the wolves.'

Klaus saw their eyes before anything else – glowing in the darkness of the tunnel. The animals bounded towards the villagers, gradually taking form as they were lit by the firebrands some of the villagers held. The firelight glittered on the metal grafted into their fur.

The first wolf leapt before it reached the cavern. It snarled in mid air, teeth snapping and oily viscous liquid dripping from its metal jaws. Klaus stood frozen to the spot as the mass of fur, metal and death hurtled towards him.

Then Caplan stepped in front, slicing sideways

with his sword. He timed it perfectly, the blade meeting the animal while it was still in the air and biting deep. The second wolf skidded to a wary halt at the end of the tunnel. Its head swayed back and forth as it regarded the shattered, dying remains of its fellow.

Finding his courage again, Klaus ran forwards, swinging his shovel. He caught the wolf a heavy blow on the snout. The beast was knocked sideways, whimpering in pain. But at once it was turning back, snarling, leaping.

This time it was one of the other villagers that came to Klaus's aid. The man thrust his burning torch into the animal's jaws. The wolf howled angrily, but it was distracted enough for Caplan to step forward and stab downwards hard with his sword.

A third wolf bounded out of the tunnel – and ran straight onto the sword of one of the other soldiers. It whimpered, and fell sideways.

Behind the distraction of the wolves, the two Plague Warriors still advanced. Other villagers were trying desperately to hold them back, but with little success. One of Caplan's guards got too close and was dealt a savage blow from a metal fist. He crashed into the wall of the cavern, head snapping back. Unconscious or dead, the Plague Warriors were already past him and there was no way to get to the man.

Klaus gestured and shouted for everyone to fall

back. As soon as they had enough distance between themselves and the lurching, nightmare figures, Caplan nodded to Klaus and he yelled for everyone to retreat.

Not too fast, or the Plague Warriors might not follow. But too slowly, and the creatures would catch them. The villagers stumbled back along the narrow tunnel, waving firebrands, trying not to trip on the scattered bones and fallen rocks that littered the uneven floor.

They were not all successful. One older man slipped, his foot shooting out from under him as he trod on a skull. The skull shattered to fragments, but the man was too slow getting up again. A metal hand closed round his ankle, squeezing tight, dragging him back.

Klaus grabbed the man's hand, desperately trying to pull him away from the Plague Warrior. But to no avail – the man disappeared back into the darkness with a scream that stopped all too abruptly.

By the time they were back at the door to the crypt they had lost another villager. It could have been a lot worse, Klaus knew, but even so he felt sick with despair.

'Something coming,' Old Nicolai gasped as Klaus hauled open the crypt door.

'Plague Warriors,' Caplan said.

Nicolai shook his head. 'From that way.' He pointed down another passageway that joined the main one just behind them.

'More wolves?' Klaus looked back, peering into the gloom. As he watched a faint light appeared, a tiny point in the darkness bobbing about in the air. It grew in size and intensity, until he could see the light came from a short rod the Doctor was holding. Klaus felt his heart lurch as he saw that Olga was beside the Doctor. She was safe.

'Gangway!' the Doctor yelled. 'Coming through – get that door open!'

As soon as they were all through, Klaus closed and bolted the door. Together with the Doctor, Caplan and the surviving guard, he hauled a stone table from the side wall across the front of the door.

'The door opens inwards, so that should keep them out,' Caplan said, gasping for breath.

'Don't you believe it,' the Doctor told them. 'It might slow them down a bit. Or else they'll just find another way.'

'Did you succeed?' Klaus was keen to know. 'Did your plan work?'

'Not altogether,' the Doctor admitted. 'Not as such. Got a new plan, actually.'

'Which is?' Caplan asked.

'A work in progress. I'll let you know.'

'And now there are dozens of Plague Warriors,' Olga said. 'They've all woken up.'

'She's exaggerating,' the Doctor said reassuringly. 'Tens, maybe. A few dozen at the most. Ish.'

Klaus was horrified. 'So they died for nothing – our friends died for nothing?!' He looked down at the bodies of Drettle and the one other villager they had managed to bring back.

'No, of course not,' the Doctor objected. 'We know what's going on down there now.'

'More Plague Warriors waking up,' Caplan said. 'That can't be a good thing.'

'It's better to know,' the Doctor told him. 'And knowledge is the greatest weapon of all.'

'So what will you do with the knowledge?' Old Nicolai demanded. 'Knowledge won't bring these people back.'

'Working on it, like I said.'

'At least we know the Cybermen are coming,' Olga pointed out.

'Forewarned is forearmed,' the Doctor agreed. 'They'll be desperate to restore power and to repair their ship. For that they need…' His voice tailed off.

At the same moment, there was a hammering on the crypt door. The wood cracked, but held.

'They need – what?' Klaus shouted above the sound. A splinter of wood flew past his face. 'Doctor – what do they need?'

The Doctor's face seemed frozen and expressionless. 'Spare parts,' he said.

A metal fist burst through the wooden door – reached through, feeling for the bolts and the obstruction.

'First part of the plan,' the Doctor announced.

'Yes?' Olga prompted.

'Get out of here – come on, everyone!'

The open grave was the most obvious route the Cybermen might use. The Doctor was convinced they would attack the village in their search for anything – and anyone – they could adapt to repair their ship.

Klaus and old Nicolai set about shovelling the earth back into the grave. Caplan sent the other guard back to the castle to ask Lord Ernhardt for reinforcements.

'We'll need all the help we can get,' the Doctor told him.

'It won't be much,' Caplan said. 'Half a dozen lads, if we're lucky. Most have never used a sword in anger.'

'They'll need to get angry soon.'

'You really think they'll come at us through the church or the graveyard?' Klaus asked.

The Doctor nodded. 'Quickest route. The only other way is out through the other side of their ship and up in the field and the woods.' He pointed through the persistent rain to the small wood on the other side of the church.

'Where you told us not to go,' Olga said.

'They won't go in there for the same reason. Radiation – it affects the Cybermen too. Not in the same way as it does humans. But it upsets their systems, messes up the intra-cybernetic communication relays. So they sort of spasm and seize up.'

'Can we use this radiation as a weapon against them?' Caplan asked.

'It's just as deadly to us, so not really.'

'But maybe we could lead them into a trap,' Klaus suggested. 'Send them into the field and the woods or something.'

'It wouldn't work. The radiation is at a dangerous level there, yes. But it won't work instantly, and as soon as they realise what's going on they'll just get out of there fast.'

'So what can we do?' Old Nicolai demanded.

'Not a lot, to be honest. Try to keep the Cybermen away from the village. Hold them back, as close to the church and their ship as we can.'

'Is that all?' Olga asked.

'It may be enough. We've got rid of their power converter, so they're back to just getting a trickle of energy from the storms. If we can hold them back long enough, make them use up enough power, then they'll have to re-energise. If they can't, then they'll return to their tombs.'

'Wear them out, and they'll go back to sleep – is that what you're saying, Doctor?' Caplan asked.

'Best I've got for the moment. But like I said, working on it.'

'It'll be dark soon,' Klaus said, looking up at the cloud-heavy sky. 'The men will need rest if they're going to have to fight the Plague Warriors again.'

'Someone needs to keep watch,' Olga said. 'You men get your beauty sleep. I'll organise some of the women to help me.'

'Help you?' Klaus said. 'You need rest too after today.'

'Like I can sleep with all this going on. Go on – you need to tell everyone what's happening and make sure they're ready.'

'They'll come at night,' the Doctor said.

'Are they nocturnal creatures then?' Old Nicolai asked.

'No. But they'll attack when you humans are at your lowest ebb, when you're tired and your senses are at their weakest. Darkness and fatigue – that's what they'll count on.'

'It's good that the rain's letting up a bit then.' Nicolai pointed to the sky, where the clouds were clearing slightly. There were patches of pale blue breaking through. 'It's almost a full moon tonight. With luck it won't get that dark.'

The moonlight struggled weakly through the clouds. The rain had eased to a drizzle, but it seeped through Olga's coat and into her clothing. She felt chilled to the bone. She was sitting on the stone wall surrounding the graveyard. It might as well have been carved from ice, the stone was so cold. But it was that or the muddy ground.

Beside her, the Doctor had jumped down from the wall. He stamped his feet and blew dragon's breath – as the village children called it – into the cold air. Olga had seen such things the last few days that she wondered if dragons were real too. The Doctor would know, but she didn't dare to ask.

She thought of Klaus snug and warm in bed. Though more likely he was sitting in the tavern, unable to sleep, as worried about Olga as she was about the Cybermen. No, that was silly – why would he be worried about *her*? Just because she worried about him didn't mean it went both ways, did it? Or did it?

'It's starting,' the Doctor whispered close to Olga's ear. 'You hear that?'

She couldn't hear anything except her own teeth chattering. Unless… No, he was right – there was something. Coming from beneath them. A rhythmic sound like someone brushing dust out of the door. She looked at the Doctor, but his attention was fixed on the graveyard in front of them.

Without warning, the Doctor jumped back up onto the wall. He stood, balancing precariously for a moment, then jumped down again, now on the other side so he was outside the graveyard.

'I think you should join me,' he told Olga. 'Best to keep out of sight.'

She swung her legs round and over the other side of the wall before pushing herself off. The Doctor caught her and gently but firmly lowered her to the ground. He put his finger to his lips and pointed back into the graveyard.

At first she could see nothing. Then the moonlight increased slightly as clouds scudded away, and Olga saw that the ground was moving. It was most obvious in the new soil packed down over Liza's grave. But even the grass was swaying, twisting, moving...

Suddenly, a silver fist punched up through the ground. The hand unclenched, fingers grasping the air. Another followed, and another. All over the graveyard, metal hands and arms thrust upwards like grotesque trees erupting from the grass.

Liza's grave was alive. Soil rolled away as the whole area heaved upwards. The hands of a Cyberman pushed through and upwards. The head followed, earth and mud falling from the black eye sockets as the creature rose up, heaving itself out of the ground.

'Get Klaus,' the Doctor said.

But Olga was unable to move. She could only stare in horror as more of the Plague Warrior Cybermen pushed their way up through the ground. They hauled themselves out into the night air, metallic bodies tarnished with mud and dirt, glinting in the cold moonlight.

Chapter 13

'Get Klaus,' the Doctor said again, his voice stern.

Olga nodded, but still she did not move.

He put his hand on Olga's shoulder. 'Go on – it'll be all right. The Cybermen need to orientate themselves. They know they're low on power, so they won't risk draining their reserves using energy weapons…' He frowned as he looked at her. 'You're not following any of this are you?'

'Yes I am. A bit.' Finally she turned to look back at him, tearing her gaze away from the sight of the Cybermen. 'No, not really.'

'Just find Klaus. Tell him the Plague Warriors are on the move. He and the others have to keep them away from the village – away from the children. Do you understand that?'

'Of course. They need to make the warriors tire, exhaust them.'

'That's right. Good girl.'

She blinked at being called a girl, especially by someone as young as the Doctor appeared to be. But he didn't seem to notice her surprise.

'And you, Olga, you stay with the children. That's where you're needed. You understand that, don't you?'

She backed away from the wall, turning to negotiate the dark path back to the village. 'I understand,' she said. But she suspected he knew she didn't believe him.

Old Nicolai and Klaus were sat together at a table in the tavern. Both had their heads down, resting on their arms which were folded on the table. Nicolai was snoring.

Klaus was awake immediately at Olga's touch. He blinked the sleep from his eyes. 'It's started.'

He wasn't asking a question, but Olga nodded in confirmation.

Nicolai snorted and woke. 'Is it time?'

'It is,' Klaus told him. 'Let's get everyone ready.'

'Hurry,' Olga said. 'We don't have long.'

'Where are you going?' Klaus called after her.

'To get all the children together.'

'You're staying with the children?' Klaus looked both surprised and relieved.

'Of course not,' Olga told him. 'I'll get them all together, and their mothers can look after them. I'll put Gretl in charge. She'll take no nonsense from any of them.' Except Heini, she thought – your own children were always the worst behaved. Or so it seemed.

The Cybermen stood like statues in the graveyard. Rain splashed off their metal armour. The first rays of the morning light glinted on the silent figures.

'What are they waiting for?' Olga asked.

'I thought you were looking after the children.'

'The children are fine.'

The Doctor nodded. 'It might not have been the children I was worrying about,' he murmured.

'Klaus wants you to talk to the men,' Olga said. 'He wants to know if they should attack.'

The Doctor shook his head. 'No point in provoking a response. The longer they just stand there, the better. Gives me more time to put my new plan into shape.'

'Into shape?'

The Doctor followed her back towards the village. They'd know soon enough if the Cybermen started to move.

'Into shape,' he said again. 'You know – work it out, add it up, decide what it sort of *is*. Really.'

'You don't actually have a new plan, do you?'

'Let's say I'm working on it. Work in progress.'

Olga hoped progress would be swift. Having seen what the Cybermen could do, she dreaded the moment they started to move, the moment they turned as one towards the village and marched out of the graveyard...

The men from the village had assembled in the street outside the tavern. There was less of a sense of bravado and excitement than there had been before the battle in the catacombs. A sense of foreboding hung over them all, reinforced by the absence of those killed or injured the previous day, and a few who were too sick with plague to help.

Old Nicolai and Klaus were standing at the front of the crowd. Klaus in particular looked relieved to see the Doctor.

'Why are we doing what he says?' a voice called out as soon as the Doctor approached.

'Yeah – he got people killed. And for what?'

'So that the rest of us can live,' Old Nicolai shouted back.

'That's right,' Klaus agreed. 'So pipe down and listen to what the Doctor's got to say.'

'What have I got to say?' the Doctor asked quietly.

'Tell them what they have to do, and why,' Olga said. 'And tell them what will happen if they don't. They're scared, and when you're scared it's easiest to do nothing. So they need to know they're doing the right thing.'

The Doctor nodded. He stepped up to stand

beside Klaus and Old Nicolai. 'You need to know that you're doing the right thing,' he called out. 'Well, you are.'

'But what are we doing?' Klaus asked quietly, when it became apparent that the Doctor thought he'd finished.

'Ah – good point.' The Doctor nodded for a moment before seeming to realise that it was a point he should address. 'Oh right – yes. There is a plague in this village. I don't just mean the disease, though that's bad enough, obviously. But *under* the village, beneath the graveyard, another poison. What you call Plague Warriors, and you're right – the Cybermen are like a plague. They poison and corrupt everything and everyone they come into contact with. They want to survive, which I suppose is fair enough, actually, but they'll go to any lengths to do it. They don't care – literally don't care, as they have no concept of emotions – about what or who gets sacrificed for their survival.'

'But what do they want from us?' someone called out.

The Doctor clicked his fingers and pointed at them. 'Ah yes, coming to that. They want whatever they can find. They're scavengers. Not just metal and bits and pieces to repair their ship, but people too. You and me. That's what they want.'

'What for?'

'To turn them into more Cybermen – more Plague

185

Warriors. Or just for spare parts. You've seen that, some of you – what they did with the bodies of the dead. They'll hunt you down – you, your friends, your children. Anything that might be useful they'll take. Anything that might be a threat to them they'll destroy. You, your village, even the land you live on. And they won't stop there – they'll spread out and infect the whole country. In time, the whole world.'

'How do we stop them?'

'Another excellent question – you guys are on fire this morning. Well, not *actually* on fire.' The Doctor glanced down at his feet. 'Sorry, probably not the most tactful allusion there. Moving on… Stop the Cybermen, the Plague Warriors, yes I think we can. At the moment they're relatively weak. They daren't use their most powerful weapons as they don't have the energy for them. Drain their power and they'll run down like… like…' He struggled to think of something it might be like that the villagers would understand.

'Like a clock?' Nicolai suggested. 'When it runs down?'

'Like a run-down clock, yes good one – bit more complicated than that, but it'll do. It's a bit more like when you get tired and need sleep, actually. Make them work too hard and they'll need to go back to sleep, or recharge. But we need to wear them out soon, before they set up more energy extraction points and build power converters out of whatever they can find.'

'Why should we believe any of this?' someone called out. It was the man who had first accused the Doctor of getting people killed. 'How do we know he has a clue about these Plague Warriors?'

Another figure pushed through the crowd to join the Doctor, Nicolai and Klaus at the front of the group. The villagers gasped. Several of them bowed their heads.

'I wonder if I can answer that?' Lord Ernhardt asked.

The Doctor gestured for him to go ahead. He had seen Ernhardt and his wife together with Caplan and several guards join the back of the group as he was speaking. Lady Ernhardt, he noticed, kept the hood of her cloak pulled up. Even so, the nearest villagers drew back slightly.

As he turned to address the villagers, Ernhardt kept one hand thrust into the pocket of his coat – a hand, the Doctor knew, was not actually there.

Ernhardt cleared his throat. 'What you all need to appreciate,' he said, 'is that the Doctor is a man of wisdom and learning. Oh, I don't suggest he can solve all our problems, but he does have a better understanding of the Plague Warriors than anyone else.'

'What about the Watchman?' someone shouted. 'What does he think?'

'The Watchman is dead,' Ernhardt said.

There was a general muttering and shuffling of feet at this news. Evidently the Watchman had been respected.

'He was killed by the Plague Warriors,' Ernhardt went on. 'And he died helping the Doctor to fight them. Make no mistake,' he went on, 'I have seen what these creatures can do, as I know have some of you. And the Doctor is right – if we do not oppose and stop them, then our whole way of life may soon be forfeit. Now…' He stepped closer to the people, lowering his voice as if he was speaking to each of them now as individuals rather than addressing the crowd, 'I can't tell you what to do. I can't order you to do as the Doctor says. But I for one have no hesitation in placing myself at his disposal. I shall do everything I can to help him, and I urge the rest of you to follow my example.'

There was silence for several moments. Then, a smattering of applause and shouts of approval.

'Doctor,' Lord Ernhardt prompted. 'Tell us what we must do.'

It started abruptly. There was no pause for the orders to get round, no hesitation at all. One moment the Cybermen were silent and still, assimilating data and waiting for strategies to compile and download. The next moment all of the Cybermen gathered in the graveyard were in motion. All turning towards the village, all stepping forward, feet slamming down into the soft earth as they marched forwards, towards their objective.

Crouched behind the wall, watching nervously through the spattering rain, one of the younger men turned and ran ahead of the advancing creatures.

'They're coming!' he yelled at the top of his voice. 'The Plague Warriors are on the move!'

Chapter 14

Since Olga refused to hide away with the children, Klaus insisted she stay with the Doctor. He seemed to think this was the safest place for her. Lord Ernhardt made the same suggestion to his wife.

Again, armed with what makeshift weapons they could find, the villagers set out for the graveyard to confront the Cybermen. The Doctor gave them advice. Some was useful – like the fact the Cybermen would be a little sluggish as their power levels were low, so speed would be to the villagers' advantage. Some was of less help – like: 'Try not to die.'

In numerical terms, the Cybermen and the villagers were fairly evenly matched. In a straight battle, the Cybermen would have destroyed their opponents without trouble. But following the

Doctor's advice, Klaus and Nicolai organised the men into small raiding parties that ran up to the advancing Cybermen, delivered a quick blow of sword, shovel, or whatever they had, then retreated rapidly.

The Cybermen retaliated by breaking into smaller groups themselves. They pursued the attackers, but as the Doctor had predicted their movements were slower and their reactions sluggish.

'This will tire them out?' Olga asked as the Doctor watched and nodded thoughtfully.

'It'll take a while,' the Doctor admitted. 'But every little bit helps. So long as they're using up more power than they're drawing from the storms.'

An ominous rumble of thunder punctuated his words.

'How long will it take to defeat them?'

'At this rate,' the Doctor said, 'several years. That's why we need another plan. Keep the Cybermen busy while I do a Plan B thing.'

'I have some questions,' Lady Ernhardt said.

'Oh, don't they always,' the Doctor muttered.

Olga raised an eyebrow. 'Women, you mean?'

'I mean humans – people. Questions, questions, questions, it's all I get.'

'Why are they doing this?' Lady Ernhardt went on. 'These Cybermen – why don't they just stay sleeping underground? Why wake and, when woken, why attack us?'

Olga looked at Lady Ernhardt. She still had the hood of her cloak pulled up, and her face was hidden in shadows. Rain dripped off the hood.

'It's what they do,' the Doctor told her. 'It's instinctive – except of course they don't have instincts any more than they have emotions. But there's a logic to it.'

'Which is?' Olga asked.

'Survival, for one thing. Any threat or potential threat must be deleted. You lot might not attack them now, but you know they're there so they're vulnerable in the future. Another reason is defence – they're spreading out to maintain a cordon round their ship. They know Worm and Drettle were scavenging bits and pieces, and they've already lost their precious power converter. They don't want you getting inside.'

'If they are concerned about what we might do inside their ship,' Lady Ernhardt said, 'then isn't that precisely where we should be?'

'Yes, well, maybe…' The Doctor's face crumpled like scrunched-up paper as he considered this. 'There's a difference between what the Cybermen might think is inconvenient enough to want to prevent, and what we need to do to stop them completely.'

'This power they need,' Olga said, 'does that come from their ship?'

'Routed through it.'

'Then that is where we can stop it, surely?'

'It's not as simple as that,' the Doctor protested. 'You have no idea.'

Lady Ernhardt fixed him with an unblinking stare. 'At the moment, Doctor, neither do you.'

The Doctor stared back, his face now set in a stern expression. 'Oh yes I do. Lots of ideas. Full of them. And here comes Idea Number One. Numero Uno. Digit the first. Wait here!'

Olga and Lady Ernhardt watched as the Doctor ran off to speak quickly with Lord Ernhardt and Klaus, who between them were coordinating the latest hit-and-run raids on the slowly advancing Cybermen.

The metal warriors were spread across the area, while the villagers tried to draw them away from the village itself. It was working up to a point, and the Cybermen had been sufficiently inconvenienced to start chasing after the attacking villagers.

There were some casualties, but so far all fairly minor. One of Caplan's soldiers had lingered too long as he swung his sword repeatedly at a Cyberman, and another had caught him a blow across the shoulders. Several villagers had cuts and bruises from glancing blows, or from falling over as they scrambled to back away.

In return, a few of the Cybermen were dented or slightly damaged. A lucky stroke from Caplan's sword severed tubing on a Cyberman's arm, and it spewed green fluid across the ground. The Cyberman was now fighting one-handed. Another had spectacularly exploded when several villagers ganged up on it and managed to knock its head violently backwards into a stone wall.

'Right, here's the plan,' the Doctor told Olga and Lady Ernhardt breathlessly as he ran back. 'Klaus and Lord Ernhardt and the others are going to lead the Cybermen after them. They've caused enough problems that if they seem to be on the run, the Cybermen will follow them.'

'But – into the village?' Olga asked. 'The children…'

The Doctor was shaking his head. 'Even if we divert most of them, the Cybermen will still send a few scouts to hunt through the village for anything useful to them. And that, sadly, includes the children. So it's up to the castle. That's the best place to defend. Everyone gets inside – including the children, everyone.'

'Everyone?' Olga checked.

'Everyone,' the Doctor confirmed. 'Except me.'

'No,' Lady Ernhardt told him. 'Everyone except *us*.'

There was no time to argue as Klaus and the others were already drawing most of the Cybermen away from the village and towards the castle. So the Doctor didn't waste time trying.

Instead he led Olga and Lady Ernhardt through the outskirts of the village so they could double back to get behind the Cybermen.

'Are they all following the other villagers?' Olga asked.

'Probably not. But most of them, I expect. Fingers crossed.'

'I hope Victor will be all right,' Lady Ernhardt said quietly.

The Doctor frowned. 'Yes, should have thought of that. Never mind, don't worry about him for now.'

'I worry about him constantly,' Lady Ernhardt said.

'It's in your nature,' the Doctor told her. 'Now, come on.'

They hurried through the small wooded area to the church wall where the Doctor and Olga had kept watch earlier. Outside the church a lone Cyberman stood amongst the gravestones and the piles of soil where its fellows had erupted from the earth.

'Funny,' the Doctor said quietly. 'I'd have expected them to leave two Cybermen at least. They like to work in pairs.'

'Why's that?' Olga wondered.

'Oh, it means one can stay on station, keeping guard while the other...' The Doctor's voice tailed off and his frown deepened.

'While the other – what?' Lady Ernhardt asked.

'While the other patrols the immediate area,' the

Doctor said. 'But let's not get too hung up about that. The chances of a patrolling Cyberman finding us must be about, ooh, the same as winning the lott—'

Olga grabbed his arm, cutting him off. 'Doctor – it found us.'

'What?' The Doctor was appalled. 'But I *never* win the lottery. Not unless I cheat and check what the numbers are going to be first.'

As he spoke, he peered through the trees to where Olga was pointing. There was a glint of silver in amongst the damp green and brown. The Doctor blinked the rain out of his eyes, and saw that the Cyberman was making its way steadily in their direction. It might not have seen them yet, but it soon would.

'Change of plan,' he whispered. 'I was hoping to get back into their ship through the church. But that'll have to wait. Instead – run!'

He set off along the side of the wall, keeping his head down so the Cyberman in the graveyard could not see them. Olga and Lady Ernhardt followed him as fast as they could manage over the rough, overgrown ground.

'I think he's seen us,' Olga gasped, catching up with the Doctor.

'I think you're right.'

From behind came the steady thump of the Cyberman's feet stamping down on the vegetation as it stalked through the wood. It thrust aside branches and ignored saplings, striding inexorably after the Doctor and his friends.

Where the wall turned to follow the outline of the churchyard, the wood started to thin out. Beyond was a field – an empty, open space with bare earth broken only by a sparse tufts of grass poking through the mud. Puddles lay across the surface, rain spattering into them.

The Doctor looked back, to see the Cyberman was gaining on them. The only way of escape was across the field to the woodland on the other side. But they'd be exposed the whole way.

'Here's hoping he doesn't decide now's the time to try out the energy levels in his blaster.'

'Doctor…' Olga cautioned.

'Not now – no time.' He grabbed her hand, reaching back to help Lady Ernhardt. 'Don't want you feeling left out. Now come on – it's squelching time!'

They ran across the field of mud. Each step went deep into the quagmire, water welling up round their ankles.

By the time they reached the middle of the field, each step was an effort. It seemed as if the mud was trying to suck them down into the ground.

The Cyberman fared no better. Being heavier, it sank even deeper into the mud. But it managed to maintain a steady untiring pace while the Doctor and the women got gradually slower and slower.

Finally, as they neared the woodland, there was more grass and the ground began to dry out.

The trees on this side of the field were not as dense or as healthy as those in the small area close to the grave yard. The branches were thin and misshapen, leaves stunted and sickly, withered and dry. The Doctor and his friends stumbled through the brittle woodland, until they collapsed on a mossy bank.

'We don't have long before he reaches us,' the Doctor said. For once he seemed out of breath, too.

'These trees,' Lady Ernhardt said, showing no sign of being out of breath, 'they look like they're dying.'

'Ah.' The Doctor looked round. 'Yes,' he said slowly. 'You were trying to tell me something just now, Olga. I have a nasty feeling I know what it was.'

She was still too breathless to reply, but pointed back towards the field they had just traversed.

'Field by the church,' the Doctor said. 'Where the Cybership crashed, and nothing grows.'

He pulled out his sonic screwdriver and held it up. The end lit up brightly and it emitted a frantic chattering sound.

The Doctor whistled through his teeth. 'Good news and bad news, people. The good news is that Cyberman's going to be in trouble soon because they don't like this type of radiation any more than humans do.'

'And the bad news?' Lady Ernhardt asked.

'The bad news was sort of implied in the "any more than humans do" bit of the good news.'

'Are we dying?' Olga finally managed to gasp.

'Not if I can help it. But yes – probably.' The Doctor rummaged in his pockets. 'Need a tablet and fast. Then we need to get out of here. Also fast. With the right medication, and so long as we don't linger, we should be fine.'

Through the sickly trees, they could see the Cyberman struggling to the edge of the field. Another few moments and it would be on more solid ground.

'Ah!' The Doctor gave a muted cry of triumph and produced a paper bag out of his jacket pocket. 'Oh. It's empty.'

'We handed out all the blue tablets,' Olga reminded him.

The Doctor had opened up the bag and was peering inside. 'Thought I kept a couple… Aha!' he declared. He pulled a small blue pill from inside the bag and gave it to Olga. 'Take it now.'

She did as she was told, and the Doctor retrieved another tablet which he ate himself.

Lady Ernhardt held out her hand. But the Doctor scrunched the bag into a ball and stuffed it back in his pocket.

'Right,' he said, 'time to get moving. The radiation will slow the Cyberman down, maybe even kill him, given enough time. But we shouldn't hang about here.'

'But – Lady Ernhardt needs a blue tablet,' Olga said.

'Please,' Lady Ernhardt said, her hand still out.

'I only had two,' the Doctor said.

Olga stared in astonishment. 'But… We should have broken them in half, or ground them up and shared them out or something – anything.'

'Why?'

'I need a tablet,' Lady Ernhardt said.

'No you don't,' the Doctor said.

Her hood had fallen back as they crossed the field. Her fair hair spilled out over her shoulders. The sunlight filtering through the clouds and the trees dappled her perfect, impossibly young features.

'But – *why*?'

The Doctor gave a short, confused laugh. 'Well – because you're not *real*.'

'What?'

'Doctor,' Olga said, 'what are you talking about?'

But the Doctor was staring back at Lady Ernhardt. 'Oh, I'm so sorry,' he said. 'You didn't know? I thought you knew.'

'What do you mean?' Lady Ernhardt asked, her voice a whisper, but not a trace of reaction on her face.

'Of course, you've had no exposure to complex mechanisms, no knowledge of robotics, only the slightest idea about clockwork. How could you know?' The Doctor paused, his face creased in sorrow before he said: 'Marie Ernhardt died soon after her son was born. Years ago.'

'No!'

'The Watchman made you.'

A single raindrop fell from a withered leaf and splashed onto Lady Ernhardt's face, tracing a line down her cheek. '*Made* me? But – my memories... My *life*...'

'All implanted somehow. You never suspected because you'd been programmed never to suspect. I am so sorry.'

Olga swallowed. How could the woman not know what she was? Was the Doctor even *right* about her? She wasn't sure if she felt sorry for the woman, or scared of her.

'The Watchman had probably found some Cyber technology even then,' the Doctor said. 'Nothing too advanced but it gave him clues, got him started. I'd guess that Marie Ernhardt died giving birth, or from complications. That might explain why her son Victor was such a sickly child.'

'Doctor!' Olga said urgently. 'The Cyberman!'

The Doctor turned from Lady Ernhardt just as the Cyberman crashed through the woods towards them. A tortured electronic burbling came from its mouth. Its arms flailed and lashed out as if the creature had lost all control over them. One metal hand connected with a tree truck, splintering the wood.

'The radiation's affected it,' the Doctor shouted above the noise. 'But it's still lethal. It'll try to kill us.'

He jumped aside as a Cyber arm whipped past his head. The Doctor grabbed Olga, pulling her after him, out of the way. But he wasn't quick enough. The Cyberman lashed out again, an uncoordinated movement, but a lethal one. The Cyberman's fist crashed towards Olga's head. There was a sickening crunch as it connected.

But not with Olga. The fist impacted on Lady Ernhardt's arm as she blocked the blow. Before the Cyberman could move, she grabbed the fist in both hands, and wrenched the arm downwards. As the Cyberman toppled, Lady Ernhardt struck it again, this time in the chest. The metal monster reeled backwards, colliding with a tree.

As it rebounded, Lady Ernhardt caught hold of the creature's head. With a violent twist, she wrenched it from the Cyberman's shoulders. Sparks exploded from the neck cavity and the Cyberman careered sideways, arms still flailing. It took a dozen steps, then collapsed to its knees before falling forwards.

'You're hurt!' Olga rushed to Lady Ernhardt.

The woman was staring down at her arm. The sleeve of her cloak had been ripped open, and there was a jagged cut across her forearm. But there was no blood.

The Doctor leaned across and pulled gently at the flap of broken skin. He folded it back like a piece of vellum, revealing the shining brass gears and cogs within the arm. Rods and levers clicked into place as Lady Ernhardt slowly flexed her automated fingers.

Chapter 15

Olga took Lady Ernhardt's hand in hers. She smoothed the artificial skin back into place. 'It means nothing.'

'On the contrary, it means everything,' Lady Ernhardt replied. She met Olga's gaze as the Doctor used his sonic screwdriver to seal the wound.

'That should do it,' he said.

'It only hides what's underneath,' Lady Ernhardt said. 'It doesn't alter it.'

'Yes, well talking about what's underneath, we need to get down to that Cybership. And there's only one Cyberman guarding the church now, so come on.'

They took a longer route back to the church, to avoid crossing the muddy field again. A storm was breaking, lightning lancing across the sky and thunder echoing round the valley. Rain pelted down, and by the time they got back to the graveyard they were drenched.

The Cyberman still stood on guard exactly where it had been. If it was aware of the fate of its comrade, it gave no hint of it.

'Power's so low they might just think he's dropped off the grid,' the Doctor murmured. He stuck out his bottom lip and blew hard in an attempt to dislodge the rain from the end of his nose. 'They don't seem to be taking any extra precautions, anyway.'

'So what do we do?' Olga asked. 'How do we get past the Cyberman?'

'I could—' Lady Ernhardt began.

But the Doctor cut her off. 'No, you couldn't. You were lucky against that other one – he was weakened by radiation poisoning and his power was depleted from trudging across a muddy field. Never thought I'd say that about a Cyberman, but there you go.'

'So how do we get past that and into the church?' Lady Ernhardt demanded. 'Do you have any idea?'

'Of course I do. I have a strategy that's worked before. Though possibly under rather different circumstances. But there's no reason why it shouldn't take care of a Cyberman.' The Doctor shook his head sending raindrops scattering from his hair. 'I'm going to bung a rock at it.'

*

The Doctor prised a stone from the wall that curtained the graveyard. He picked one that was about the size of an egg and fitted snugly in his palm. He tossed it from hand to hand to test the weight.

'You're sure this is a good idea?' Olga asked him.

'Ask me again in five minutes.'

'You're really just going to throw that at the Plague Warrior?' Lady Ernhardt asked.

'Really. I throw it from here, then run and join you two over there.' He pointed to the other side of the graveyard. 'Where you'll be waiting.'

'If you say so,' Olga agreed.

'I do say so.'

'You propose to draw the machine man over to this side of the graveyard so we can slip into the church behind it,' Lady Ernhardt summarised.

The Doctor gave her a big, smiley thumbs-up. 'Bingo.'

As plans went, the Doctor was later able to reflect, this one did quite well right up until the point where he threw the rock. Olga and Lady Ernhardt made their way carefully and quietly round the wall to the far side of the graveyard. They were helped by the pummelling rain which reduced visibility considerably. The rain was so heavy that even the Cyberman's infrared capabilities would be disoriented, the Doctor thought.

He waited until he was pretty sure they were in the right place, though it was difficult for him to see through the rain, too. And he couldn't just stick his head up over the wall to check or the Cyberman might see him too soon.

After what seemed like more than enough time, the Doctor stood up, took careful aim at the metal figure, hurled his rock at it… and missed. The rock shot past the Cyberman, and carried on until it clattered against the wall of the graveyard behind it. Close to where the Doctor had sent the women.

Immediately, the Cyberman jerked into life. It turned towards the sound, and marched across to investigate. In front of it, Olga's face appeared above the wall as she looked to see what had happened. She disappeared again at once, but the Cyberman had seen her. It quickened its pace.

The Doctor grabbed another rock, and threw that. It glanced off the Cyberman's shoulder, but the creature did not deviate from its course. Rather than try again to distract it, the Doctor ran. Head down, he charged through the rain along the side of the wall – and collided with Lady Ernhardt coming the other way. Olga was right behind her.

'Change of plan,' the Doctor announced. 'Over the wall and into the church while he's looking the other way, come on.' He laced his hands to make a step for Lady Ernhardt, but she had already jumped up onto the wall, pulling Olga after her.

'Not sure I'm really needed here,' the Doctor muttered, scrambling up after them.

The Cyberman was still on the other side of the graveyard. It didn't stop at the wall, but crashed through the precarious structure, sending stones flying in all directions. It turned quickly one way, then the other, hunting its prey.

But the Doctor and his friends were already inside the church, shaking the rain from their hair and hurrying down towards the crypt.

'That was easy,' the Doctor said brightly. 'Now for the tricky part.'

The door from the back of the crypt into the catacombs had been smashed apart by the Cybermen as they broke through into the church. The floor was strewn with splintered wood. The Doctor, Olga, and Lady Ernhardt picked their way through the debris and out into the catacombs.

'Hope I can remember the way,' the Doctor joked. But neither of his companions reacted.

They made their way through the tunnels, the Doctor's sonic screwdriver lighting the way. Every so often, they paused and listened for any sound that might suggest they were not alone.

'You think there will be more Cybermen down here?' Olga asked.

'They won't have left their ship unguarded,' the Doctor told her. 'The question is, how many? And can we get past them?'

'That's two questions,' Lady Ernhardt pointed out.

'And just how pedantic should one be in these sorts of situations?' the Doctor went on, as if he hadn't heard her.

The Doctor's caution seemed infectious. As they approached the area where the ship was buried, they slowed down and spoke in whispers. Finally, they arrived in the large cavern where the villagers had battled against the Cybermen.

'No bodies,' the Doctor noted, holding up the sonic screwdriver.

'Is that a good thing?' Lady Ernhardt wondered.

'Depends who took them, and what they've done with them.'

'There are no guards,' Olga whispered.

'Not that we can see,' the Doctor agreed. 'Cybermen aren't arrogant by nature, but maybe their resources are stretched a bit thin and they really have sent every available Cyberman to secure the village.' He caught sight of Olga's expression. 'Don't worry, everyone will be fine up in the castle. The only way in is over that narrow bridge across the ravine and...' He hesitated, a frown deepening across his face.

'Except, that's not the only way in,' Olga said.

'There is access from these tunnels,' Lady Ernhardt said.

'And the Cybermen know about it,' the Doctor said. 'One of them was in the Watchman's laboratory.' He slapped his palm hard against his forehead. 'Think – why don't I think? I should have thought of that.'

'You were preoccupied,' Olga told him. 'None of us thought of it.'

'No excuse!' The Doctor took a deep breath and turned a complete circle on the spot. 'Right, I have things to sort out on the Cybership, then we get to the castle and warn them. And block off the tunnels.'

'Should we go on to the castle ahead of you?' Olga asked.

'Do you know the way?'

Both women shook their heads.

'Probably not a good idea, then. You'd better stick with me.'

They left the cavern, and took the tunnels that led to the fractured side of the ship.

'Won't they expect us to come in this way?' Olga asked. She was aware they had entered this way twice already.

'Doubt it. They don't know how we got in before. You wait here, and I shan't be two ticks.'

'Wait here? Why wait here?' Olga asked.

'I'll be quicker on my own. And you can warn me if lots of Cybermen come back.'

'You think they will return?' Lady Ernhardt asked.

'Once they find they can't get into the castle above ground, they might send a force back this way to try from underneath, yes.'

'Unless they have already started an assault from these tunnels.'

The Doctor shook his head. 'Oh you're a bundle of optimism, aren't you, missy?' He raised his hand, holding up three fingers. 'Like I said – two ticks.'

He handed Olga the sonic screwdriver. Then he ducked into the red-lit Cybership and disappeared along the corridor inside.

'He knows what he is doing,' Olga said.

As she spoke, the Doctor again passed the hole in the ship wall, this time heading the other way down the corridor.

The gates of the castle were closed and barred. They shuddered under the impact of blows from the other side, but so far they were withstanding the assault.

From the battlements, Klaus, Nicolai and Lord Ernhardt looked down at the narrow bridge across the precipice. They had discussed whether it could be destroyed before the Cybermen arrived, but there was no time and the bridge was solid stone, strong and robust.

'You think they'll get in?' Klaus asked.

He had counted almost thirty of the metal warriors. Most of them stood on the bridge, just watching while a handful hammered on the gates. It was as many as could get close enough to be effective.

'Eventually, they will,' Lord Ernhardt said. 'But how long we have before the gates give way, I don't know.'

'Perhaps they'll wear themselves out before they get through,' Nicolai said. 'Maybe that's the Doctor's plan.'

The gatehouse beneath them shook under another onslaught.

On the bridge, half of the watching Cybermen slowly turned and started back down the cliff path.

'Giving up?' Klaus wondered.

'Or getting something to use as a battering ram,' Nicolai suggested.

'No,' Lord Ernhardt said, his face pale. 'They didn't know where we were going or what we were planning when they followed us here.'

'So – now they do,' Klaus said.

'Exactly. They have us trapped in the castle. And they know there's another way in.' Lord Ernhardt turned and hurried down the steps to ground level. 'Come on – there's no time to lose. We have to collapse the tunnels!'

'Gangway – coming through!'

They heard the Doctor long before they saw his shadow in the red lighting within the corridor. They also heard the distinctive tread of the Cybermen following him.

The Doctor leaped through the hole in the side of

the ship, grabbing his sonic screwdriver from Olga's hand as he passed.

'Well, come on!' he yelled as he ran.

Olga looked back as they reached the end of the tunnel. The first Cyberman was clambering through the gap in the ship's hull. One hand either side, it pulled itself through and straightened up. Blank eyes stared straight at her.

'Did you achieve what you set out to do?' Lady Ernhardt was asking as Olga caught them up again.

'I hope so. Managed to dodge the Cyberboys till the last minute. But I think we're clear of them now.'

They reached an intersection of tunnels, and the Doctor chose one that sloped upwards – towards the castle, Olga guessed.

'Are we safe yet?' she asked.

'Never safe with Cybermen about. But yes, probably. I think. Should be. For a while.'

A huge dark shape loomed out of a side passageway. A metal fist punched through the air, just missing the Doctor's head and embedding itself in the rock wall.

'Or not,' the Doctor decided. 'Come on!'

They raced on again. Maybe it was her imagination, but Olga thought she recognised the tunnel now. Was it wishful thinking, or were they close to the castle?

'What is that?' Lady Ernhardt asked.

'What? Can't see anything,' the Doctor said.

'No – listen.'

Olga could hear it too. A low rumble, coming from the tunnel ahead of them.

'No idea,' the Doctor said, and Olga knew instinctively that he was lying. 'But I think we'd better hurry.'

The tunnel became steeper, and there were lamps fixed to the walls now. In most of them, the oil had been used up. But a few still burned with a flickering, guttering flame.

They rounded another corner, and the Doctor skidded to a halt.

Olga and Lady Ernhardt piled into the back of him, knocking him forwards.

'What is it?' Olga gasped. 'Why have you stopped?'

'Tunnel's blocked,' the Doctor said. He took out his sonic screwdriver again and shone it ahead of them. The tunnel was filled with rock and rubble.

'It wasn't like that before,' Olga said. 'We came this way – I know we did.'

'Has the roof collapsed?' Lady Ernhardt asked.

The Doctor shook his head. 'This is deliberate. Your husband must have realised the Cybermen could get into the castle this way. Clever man.'

Lady Ernhardt nodded. 'He is. Very clever.'

'Too clever by half in this case.'

'What do you mean? He has stopped the Cybermen.'

'Slowed them down maybe. They'll just dig through that lot when they get here. And that won't be long.'

The ground was shaking under their feet – a steady, rhythmic thump of marching feet.

'I reckon there's about ten of them coming,' the Doctor said.

'We must double back, find another way,' Olga said. She grabbed the Doctor's arm to pull him away from the blockage.

'There isn't another way. We're too close now, this is the only tunnel that goes into the castle. In any case,' the Doctor went on, 'the Cybermen are too close. They're already past the last turnoff.'

Olga looked round, eyes wide with fear. 'Then – where can we go? If there are Cybermen behind us and the passage is blocked ahead?'

'Only forwards,' Lady Ernhardt said. 'If the Doctor is right, there is no other way.'

'And the way ahead is blocked,' the Doctor said. 'We're trapped.'

He led them back round the last bend in the tunnel and shone the sonic screwdriver back down the way they had come. Something glittered in the pale light.

A dark shape loomed out of the blackness, other shapes behind it. The tunnel floor was still shaking as the Cybermen advanced, the flickering light of a failing lamp glinting on their implacable silver armour as they strode up the tunnel towards the Doctor and his friends.

The leading Cyberman raised its hand, pointing along the passageway at them.

'Delete. Delete. Delete,' it rasped.

Chapter 16

The passageway opened out slightly at the rock fall. Even so, Lady Ernhardt had to push past Olga and then the Doctor to proceed along the tunnel.

'It's no use,' Olga told her. 'There's no way past.'

'There will be,' Lady Ernhardt insisted. She grabbed one of the fallen stone slabs from the roof and lifted it away. Other rocks and debris fell to take its place.

'There isn't time to dig through,' Olga insisted.

The Cyberman were advancing along the tunnel towards them. It was only wide enough where they were to allow the huge metal warriors to proceed in single file. But that would be enough. Olga knew what would happen in a few moments when the Cybermen reached them.

'No, no, no,' the Doctor said. 'Marie's right – I can call you Marie, can't I?' He didn't wait for an answer. 'Thanks.'

'But the Cybermen,' Olga said, as Marie hefted aside another heavy slab of stone as if it was a pebble. Again more debris shifted – there was now the narrowest gap at the top of the pile. But not enough to get through.

'Same plan as before.' The Doctor grabbed one of the slabs that Marie had pushed aside. 'Blimey – that's heavy.' He lifted it with an effort, raising it above his head. 'Get behind me, Olga.'

She pushed past, wondering what he intended.

'Like before – we bung rocks at them!'

It wasn't much of a throw. But the stone slab was heavy, and the ground sloped down towards the advancing Cybermen. The makeshift projectile rolled and bounced down the tunnel, and cracked into the leading Cyberman, sending it staggering backwards.

But it wasn't damaged – merely delayed. It stepped over the slab, and continued towards them.

'Keep working at the blockage,' the Doctor told Marie. 'Olga – push the rocks back towards me. Not too big, but big enough to be useful.'

As Marie frantically pulled at the rocks blocking the passage, and Olga rolled them back towards the Doctor, the gap at the top of the fallen pile of rubble grew slowly bigger. There was light – faint flickering light – shining through from the next section of tunnel.

The Doctor gathered up rocks as they reached him, and hurled them at the approaching Cybermen. Some of the rocks missed their targets completely. But others clanged into the leading Cyberman, leaving it battered and dented. The creature struggled on, making slow headway against the blizzard of stones and rocks. But it was edging slowly, steadily closer.

At last, the gap at the top of the rubble was large enough that they might – just – be able to squeeze through.

'You must go first,' Marie told Olga. When the woman hesitated, Marie added: 'I am still clearing the rocks, and the Doctor is keeping the Plague Warriors back. It must be you. See if it is clear at the top, or if not then you must dig through to the other side.'

Olga nodded, too frightened to answer. The Cybermen had almost reached the Doctor, who was backing slowly up to the edge of the fallen debris. The leading Cyberman's armour was blackened and dented. One of the metal rods on the side of its head had snapped after taking a direct hit, and green fluid dripped out and over its shoulders. But still it was advancing on them...

With a nod of urgent encouragement from the Doctor, Olga clambered up the pile of fallen rubble. It shifted and moved under her feet. She sank in, like in the muddy field by the church, but somehow she managed to scramble to the top.

A strip of darkness, with just the faintest of flickering lights coming from somewhere deep inside. Olga reached in, probing, feeling, scrabbling. She forced her head and shoulders through the gap, arms out in front of her.

Then a dark shape moved in front of the faint light, blotting it out. Something grabbed her hands, and Olga screamed.

Caplan had been left in charge of the defences at the gates. He organised his few men so that half were stationed inside the gates, the others on the battlements above the gatehouse.

The Cybermen had a new tactic. While continuing to batter at the gates – and make some progress as the wood weakened under the onslaught – they were also climbing up the walls. It was slow, but the creatures seemed to have infinite reserves of patience. They moved methodically, metal fingers working their way into any cracks in the solid façade of the castle. Where there was no handhold, they made one, punching and gouging into the solid rock face.

The first Cyberman was nearing the top of the battlements. But Caplan was waiting for it. He too could be patient. If he struck too soon he would be at a disadvantage, leaning down and off balance. It was not until the Cyberman was almost on him before he delivered an almighty blow with his sword.

Caplan's blade slammed into the Cyberman's upper body, knocking it backwards. But it managed to hold on. Caplan followed up with a thrust – the tip of the broad sword right into the creature's head. Already off balance, the blow was enough. The head snapped back. An arm lashed out, almost catching Caplan, but he stepped aside at the last instant.

Then the Cyberman was falling backwards. It tumbled down the side of the castle wall, catching another of the metal warriors as it fell, dislodging that one too. Both of them fell – one smashing down on the stone-flagged floor outside the gatehouse, close to the Cybermen attacking the gates. The other Cyberman missed the bridge, and fell into the ravine.

Caplan didn't see where it landed. He was watching the Cyberman lying on its back far below by the main gates. Watching it haul itself to its feet, and start climbing back up the wall.

'Easy – easy!'

Olga recognised the voice, and her heart leaped. She stopped fighting the hands that had grabbed her in relief and surprise.

'Klaus!'

'Who else would it be?'

She allowed herself to be pulled through the narrow gap, over the rough debris, and out onto the other side. Klaus lifted her down, holding her for a moment before turning back to the pile of rubble.

'Who's with you?'

'The Doctor, and Lady Ernhardt.'

Another figure stepped out of the near darkness. 'Marie? She's all right?' Lord Ernhardt asked urgently.

Olga wasn't sure how to answer that. Did he know what his wife truly was? Surely he must – but there again, she had not known it herself.

But he didn't wait for her answer, pushing past and clambering up the pile of debris to help Klaus pull Marie Ernhardt through from the other side.

'Victor – how is Victor?' she gasped as soon as she was through.

'He's fine,' Lord Ernhardt assured her. 'Fine. Sleeping peacefully.' He pulled her into an awkward embrace, balanced precariously on the side of the mountain of rubble. 'I was so worried about you, Marie.' He helped her down to join Olga.

The Doctor was almost through the gap when his face creased up in pain. 'It's got my leg,' he cried.

Klaus was pulling at the Doctor's arms. Lord Ernhardt checked his wife was safely down, then scrambled back up to help Klaus. The Doctor was now fully through, but a metal arm was reaching through after him, holding his ankle. Klaus hammered at it with a piece of rock – the sound echoing off the tunnel walls.

Marie started to climb back up, but before she was halfway, the Doctor broke free. He shot forward, Klaus and Lord Ernhardt falling back. The Doctor rolled and tumbled rapidly down the pile with a cry of 'Geronimo!' and landed at Olga's feet.

She helped him up, and he smiled a thank you. Then he was immediately climbing back up again.

'Back! Back! Everyone get back!' he yelled.

'But – they're coming through,' Klaus protested.

The first Cyberman was hauling itself through the gap. Arms and head were already visible. Its blank eyes stared at the humans waiting for it.

'That's why you have to get back,' the Doctor shouted. He grabbed Klaus by the shoulders and thrust him backwards. 'You too,' he told Lord Ernhardt.

'But, what can you do?' Olga called up after him.

The Doctor raised his sonic screwdriver. 'However you brought down the roof, I'm hoping its weakened the structure above. A bit of well-aimed sonic agitation, and…'

His words were blotted out by a high-pitched whine. The sonic screwdriver glowed brightly.

The Cyberman was almost through. It started to clamber to its feet, right next to the Doctor. In moments it would be on him.

A patter of dust scattered across the Cyberman's shoulders. It ignored it and reached for the Doctor. But he was already sliding down the rubble on his backside, sonic screwdriver still aimed.

The patter became a trickle, and then several chunks of rock dislodged from above. They clanged against the Cyberman's armour as they fell. Another Cyberman was reaching through the gap. It raised its head to look upwards – just as the roof collapsed.

An avalanche of rock and rubble crashed down, closing the gap and burying the Cyberman who was halfway through. The Cyberman standing stooped against the roof at the top of the pile was knocked to its knees, then forwards onto its face. Dust filled the tunnel, and rocks and stones clattered down, forcing the Doctor and the others to run back up the passageway.

The dust had blown out the remaining lamps. The only light was from the now-silent sonic screwdriver. The tunnel was now filled with a solid wall of densely packed rubble. Near the top, a silver hand projected from the debris. The fingers clenched and spasmed for a few moments. Then they were still.

'It will take them a while to get through there,' the Doctor said. He wiped the back of his grubby hand across his grimy face, smearing dust across his features.

'But they will try,' said Marie.

'Yes,' the Doctor agreed. 'They will try. Here, and at the main gates.'

*

The main gates were creaking under the constant strain of the Cybermen's assault. The Cybermen seemed to have given up on climbing over the walls. Looking down, Caplan saw that instead they were attacking the areas beside the gates, hammering their fists into the stonework.

'Are they trying to weaken the gates?' the guard beside Caplan asked.

'They could be trying to get at the hinges,' he agreed. 'Or maybe they're just scraping their way through the walls. Either way, it doesn't look good.'

'What doesn't look good?'

Caplan turned, relieved to hear Lord Ernhardt's voice. He was surprised but pleased to see that the Doctor was with him. Caplan quickly explained what the Cybermen were up to.

'They only need to make the smallest hole in the wall or the gates, and they'll be inside in no time,' the Doctor said.

'Then what do we do? How do we stop them?'

The Doctor looked up at the dark sky. More storm clouds were gathering. Thunder echoed round the castle courtyard.

'Well, I do have an idea. But first let's get everyone somewhere safe.'

'We can't get out of the castle,' Caplan pointed out. 'And where will be safe if they can get in *here*?'

'The catacombs,' the Doctor told him. 'Get everyone down into the tunnels. The way back to the village is blocked, but maybe you can hide down there for long enough for me to deal with the Cybermen.'

'You think you can?' Lord Ernhardt asked.

'I have the gleam of a hint of the start of an idea. Just get everyone down in the tunnels and keep them safe.'

Lord Ernhardt nodded and turned to his guard captain. 'Caplan – assemble everyone by the Watchman's workshop. I must go to Marie, she's with Victor. We need to move him too.'

'Victor!' The Doctor slammed his palm into his forehead. 'Your son – I was forgetting. He could be the key to this.'

'Doctor – he's barely alive.' Lord Ernhardt's expression was grave. There was a catch in his voice as he said: 'I doubt he will survive the day.'

'I think he's more robust than you give him credit for. Come on!'

Olga sat with Marie beside the bed. Lady Ernhardt's first thought as they emerged from the tunnels had been for her son. Olga didn't understand how someone who was artificial could have such feelings. But she had witnessed how the mothers of the children she taught felt about them, and she saw the same love and anxiousness in Marie Ernhardt.

The woman had a child, and loved him. It was simple. And perhaps that made her more human than Olga…

The young man in the bed seemed exactly as he had been when Olga had seen him before. It was possible that he hadn't even moved. He remained pale and still, the bed covers pulled up to his chin.

They sat in silence for several minutes. They were still sitting there, watching Victor Ernhardt's pale features, when Lord Ernhardt and the Doctor joined them.

'Marie, my love – we have to move him,' Ernhardt said gently. He put his hand on his wife's shoulder. The cuff of his other sleeve flapped empty at his side.

'We cannot,' she said, without looking away from her son's prone figure in the bed. 'The Watchman's instructions are clear.'

'The Watchman is dead,' the Doctor told her shortly. Olga raised her eyebrows, but the Doctor ignored her. 'We can't leave him here for the Cybermen.'

'Caplan is getting everyone into the tunnels for safety,' Ernhardt explained. 'We might be safe here, but I suspect not.'

'I shall stay with him. I'll protect him,' Marie insisted.

'My Lady,' Olga said gently. 'Marie – you can't just stay here with him alone.'

'Why not?'

'Because if you do,' the Doctor said, 'who will protect you from *him*?'

As he spoke, he stepped up to the bed. Marie Ernhardt cried out, reaching to stop him as he grabbed the covers. But she was too late. The Doctor threw back the sheets and blankets to reveal the young man lying there.

Olga screamed.

Lord Ernhardt took a step backwards, crossing himself. His wife's mouth dropped open. Only the Doctor did not seem surprised.

Beneath the covers, Victor Ernhardt had the body of a Cyberman. A human head on top of a body pieced together from the salvaged remains of several Cybermen. A mechanical Frankenstein's monster.

From above came the distant sound of the castle gates being smashed open. Shouts and screams. Running feet.

Victor Ernhardt sat up suddenly. His eyes opened. Around the irises, where there should have been milky white, his eyes were flecked with silver.

Chapter 17

The courtyard was in turmoil. The main gates were shattered and broken, hanging off their hinges. The walls either side had collapsed where the Cybermen forced their way through.

Now the silver warriors were moving through the courtyard, hunting down anyone they could find. Caplan and the guards did their best to hold the Cybermen back, while keeping out of range of their lethal blows.

Klaus and Nicolai hurried the children and their mothers through the inner gates and down the steps towards the catacombs. At any moment they expected to hear the tread of the Cybermen coming after them. Expected to turn a corner and find a Cyberman waiting for them.

'Where's my daddy?' Jedka demanded. 'I want my daddy. He should be here to look after us.'

'I'm sure he's fine,' Klaus assured her. 'He probably has other people to look after.'

Jedka glared at him, and Klaus realised that maybe he'd not given the best answer. 'He'll be here soon, I'm sure.'

Olga was so much better at this than him – where was she? He prayed she was safe.

'Back – everyone get back!' the Doctor warned.

Victor took a hesitant step forwards. It was an awkward, uncoordinated movement, as if he was getting used to his body.

'Victor?' Marie Ernhardt said. She made to go to him, but her husband pulled her back.

'I'm not sure it is Victor any more,' he said. His forehead was creased with sorrow.

'Why has he woken?' Olga wondered. 'Why now?'

'Because the Cybermen are nearby and in force,' the Doctor explained. 'He's caught up in the system, become part of their network. He's drawing power from it, like the other Cybermen. Somewhere in that mishmash of circuitry the Watchman has included a network link.' He raised his sonic screwdriver. 'And I've got to break it, or he'll kill us all.'

The tip of the screwdriver lit up, and it let out a high-pitched whine. Victor seemed to sag, his head lolling sideways.

'No!' the boy's mother screamed, and threw herself at the Doctor. She knocked his hand aside, and the sonic screwdriver clattered to the floor. 'I won't let you harm him!'

'I'm not harming him – I'm saving him!'

But Marie held on tight to the Doctor, pushing him away from her son.

Olga hurried forward to scoop up the sonic screwdriver. It was still operating, so she aimed it at Victor. 'I'm sorry, Marie,' she breathed. 'So sorry.'

With a grunt of pain, Victor sank to his knees. There was an echoing clang as metal made contact with stone. Slowly, he raised his head, and the silver flecks had gone from his eyes. He stared across at Marie, as she held the Doctor back.

His voice was a metallic rasp, but filled with emotion and feeling that no Cyberman could ever have. 'Mother?!'

'That's better!' The Doctor shook himself free from Marie. 'Well, don't just stand there – give him a hug.' He nudged the astonished Lord Ernhardt. 'You too, Ernie. Go for it, go on.'

'What have you done?' Olga asked as she and the Doctor watched the tentative embrace of parents and child.

'I broke the link, separated him from the Cybermen's network. Cut him loose. Gave him his freedom. Well – up to a point.'

'He will be all right?'

The Doctor sighed. 'Oh, I doubt it. But unless we get moving, none of us will be all right.'

He clapped his hands together for attention. Once everyone was looking, the Doctor went on: 'Right – here's the plan. Olga, you go and help with the children. Keep away from any Cybermen, though, right?'

'I should stay with you,' she protested.

'No,' Lord Ernhardt told her. 'Your children need you.'

'*My* children?'

'Yours as much as anyone's,' the Doctor said. 'They need you. They respect you. They love you. Right,' he went on before Olga could respond to this, 'Lord Ernie – you too. The villagers respect you as well. So you and the Mrs help Olga and the others get everyone down into the tunnels and keep them safe.'

'Very well,' Lord Ernhardt agreed.

His wife nodded. 'Come with us, Victor.'

'Um, no, actually,' the Doctor said. He smiled apologetically. 'Victor's coming with me. I need his help if we're to defeat the Cybermen.'

Lord Ernhardt frowned, but he nodded. 'Very well, Doctor.'

'He can go with you,' Marie agreed. 'But I am coming too.'

*

The Cybermen were advancing across the courtyard. Gustav, the tavern keeper, lay in a crumpled heap beside the wall. He'd got too close to a Cyberman and paid the price. Henri was dabbing at the man's wounded forehead with a damp cloth.

Caplan had organised his few remaining guards into a line across the area. They struggled to hold the Cybermen back, but were being steadily forced to retreat. Caplan whirled round as the Doctor, Marie and Victor emerged from a doorway behind. He stared in confusion at Victor.

'It's all right,' the Doctor shouted above the sound of sword on Cyber-armour. 'He's on our side.'

'I hope you know what you're doing,' Caplan said.

'I know exactly what I'm doing,' the Doctor told him. 'I'm taking Victor and we're climbing to the highest point of the castle. Er – where is that, by the way?'

Caplan pointed to one of the towers that rose above the courtyard. 'That's the highest.'

The Doctor shielded his eyes from the ever-present rain and peered up at the tower. It was on the other side of the attacking Cybermen. 'Is that a flagpole up there? Ideal. I don't suppose there's a way up there without getting past our friends?'

'None,' said Caplan.

'That figures. All right, Caplan – you and Lady Ernhardt get us past the Cybermen, and then make sure they don't follow us.'

'Lady Ernhardt?' Caplan said, surprised. 'But – this fight is no place for my Lady.'

'Quite right. I'm coming with you,' Marie said.

'No,' the Doctor insisted. 'You want to keep Victor safe? You make sure we get up there unharmed.' He turned to Caplan before she could argue. 'And don't worry – Victor's mum is quite capable of looking after herself, and probably you too. Now, the rest of your men need to protect the villagers. Lord Ernhardt and Olga have gone to help them.'

The Cybermen were slower than they had been. The Doctor guessed they were getting low on power – but nowhere near low enough to have to return to their hibernation chambers. The cost of tiring them that much would be way too high, he thought.

With Caplan swinging his sword at the nearest Cybermen, and Marie taking them on hand-to-hand, the two forged a path for the Doctor and Victor to hurry through to the base of the tallest tower. The Doctor shoved Victor through in front of him – though his shove probably went unnoticed by the young man who was almost all Cyberman. The Doctor followed, slamming and bolting the door behind them.

'For all the good that will do,' he murmured.

'What is the plan?' Victor asked. He had the inflection of a normal human being, but his voice was a metallic rasp.

'Get to the top. Do something clever,' the Doctor said. 'In that order.'

They had barely started up the curving stairway when they heard the splintering sound of the door below being smashed open.

The sound of the battle above filtered through to the tunnels. Klaus and Lord Ernhardt ushered the villagers along. Olga tried to keep the children in order. Most were with their parents, but some seemed to prefer being with her.

Jedka reluctantly held her mother's hand. 'Where's Daddy?' she demanded yet again.

'He's busy, my darling.' Her mother looked at Olga appealingly.

'I haven't seen him, not for a while,' Olga said. She couldn't lie and say the man was all right. She simply didn't know.

'He can take care of himself,' Jedka's mother assured the girl.

Jedka glared at her. 'I know that, Mummy. But I want him to take care of *us*.'

They closed every door behind them as they went. But Olga knew it would not be enough. If the Doctor's plan – whatever it was – failed, then sooner or later they would all die. Or worse, she thought, remembering the human limbs attached to cybernetic bodies, recalling Victor Ernhardt…

*

The steps seemed to go on for ever. The Doctor wasn't tired, not yet. But Victor was slowing noticeably. The good news was that all the Cybermen would be slowing, too, as their power was slowly depleted.

But without Victor, there was no point in the Doctor getting to the top of the tower. So he did his best to encourage the young man – he had to think of him as a man, despite what had been done to him. He was a human with a cybernetic body, not a Cyberman with a human head.

Except that the Doctor knew what he was planning to do to him, and it was something he could only do to a Cyberman…

Finally, they emerged onto the rain-swept platform at the top of the tower. Storm clouds were rolling in and thunder rumbled round the sky.

'The Cybermen seeded a huge storm,' the Doctor shouted above the thunder. 'It's taken a while to build, but it's coming now. So it's a good job their power converter isn't working or we'd be in real trouble.'

'We are in real trouble,' Victor grated back at him. 'What must we do?'

The Doctor was holding on to a rusted metal flagpole secured to the centre of the platform. If he let go, he thought there was a real possibility he might get blown over the parapets. Grasping it with one hand, he rummaged through his pockets with the other.

'Got some bits of the power converter here. Thought they might come in handy.'

He pulled out various components, sorting through until he found what he needed. He held them against the metal flagpole.

'Here – give me a hand. Hold these in place while I fix them there and wire them up.'

Victor seemed unaffected by the incoming storm. He stood defiantly, rain lashing down his metal body as he held the equipment where the Doctor had shown him. The Doctor set to work with the sonic screwdriver, and soon everything was secured – a mishmash of componentry held together by broken wires and frayed cables.

'What now?' Victor asked as the Doctor inspected his handiwork.

'Now we need the lightning to strike the pole. Well, just one other adjustment.' He turned from the flagpole, and raised the sonic screwdriver. 'And that's an adjustment to you – I'm sorry.'

'What are you doing?' Victor sounded interested rather than concerned.

'I've rigged a sort of bypass power converter. It will flow the power by induction into a suitable receptacle. But not until it's stored up a vast amount. It won't be a steady stream of energy to power the Cybermen – it will be a sudden blast. I've disabled the safety cut-outs on their ship's systems, so I hope the blast will destroy them.'

'And how do I help with this?'

'I have to flow the power into the Cyber network. And to do that I need to adapt a Cyberman as an input channel. A dead one or some components of one won't do, as they cut off the connections. So it needs to be a working, conscious Cyberman.'

'And that will kill the rest of the Cybermen?'

The Doctor nodded. 'Sure will.'

'Will it…' Victor hesitated. 'Will it kill me?'

'Honest answer?' The Doctor finished his sonicing. 'I don't know.'

Victor nodded his human head. 'Thank you.'

'Thank you? For what?'

'For an honest answer.'

If the Doctor had anything to say to this, he didn't get the chance. A Cyberman stood in the doorway from the stairs. It stepped out onto the roof. Lightning stabbed through the sky, and the flagpole sizzled with energy. The components the Doctor had fitted glowed and hummed into life.

Behind the Cyberman came another. They marched towards where the Doctor and Victor stood watching.

'Not enough power yet,' the Doctor said quietly. 'We need more lightning. More time.'

'You will come with us,' the first Cyberman said.

'Why?' the Doctor demanded.

'You display knowledge and intelligence beyond these other primitive humans. You are of value to us.' The Cyberman turned to Victor. 'You will be fully converted. You will be like us.'

'No,' Victor said. 'I will never be like you.'

'You have no choice.'

The storm was growing rapidly. Rain sheeted down, drenching the Doctor and cascading down the Cybermen's armour. Another bolt of lightning struck the top of the tower.

'Felt the heat of that,' the Doctor said. 'Not long now. I hope.'

'You will come now.' The Cybermen reached out for Victor and the Doctor.

'No – leave them alone!'

The shout came from the top of the stairs. Marie Ernhardt hurried out onto the roof. 'Get away from my son!'

But the Cybermen ignored her. One of them grabbed Victor's metal arms. The other closed in on the Doctor.

Victor fought back, but he was held tight – however the Watchman had assembled his body, it was weaker than the other Cybermen. Marie grabbed the Cyberman, prising its grip away from Victor's arms. Victor was knocked aside, crashing into the wall. One of the parapets broke away under the impact, the stone crashing down into the courtyard far below.

For a moment, Victor teetered on the edge of the tower. One foot slipped back, into space. Then Marie rushed across and grabbed his flailing metal arm. She heaved him back to safety.

The Cyberman she had been grappling with was close behind her. It reached for Victor again, arms about to close on him in a deadly embrace. But Marie grabbed it, dragged it away. The Cyberman turned, lashing out. The blow caught the woman across the shoulders, knocking her backwards. She clutched at the arm as she fell – dragging the Cyberman with her. Dragging it over the edge of the tower.

Locked together, the two figures fell through the gap in the broken parapet and disappeared from sight.

'No!' Victor shouted.

But they were gone.

More Cybermen emerged from the stairway and advanced across the storm-swept roof. Two of them grabbed Victor.

'Doctor?' the metal man implored.

Lightning split the sky. Thunder echoed round the valley.

'That should do it!' With a tremendous effort, the Doctor pulled himself away from the Cyberman holding him and watched as the indicator lights on his makeshift power converter showed that it had reached maximum capacity.

'Brace yourself, Victor,' he yelled.

And nothing happened.

Chapter 18

If the Cybermen were becoming slowly more sluggish, Victor now seemed re-energised. But the Doctor warned him to do nothing – for the moment.

'You might destroy a few,' he whispered as the Cybermen led the two of them back down the tower stairway, 'but we need to get them all.'

'Your plan did not work.' Victor's voice was flat – almost as emotionless as a Cyberman. 'My mother is dead.'

'She wasn't—' The Doctor broke off. Probably not the best time to tell a half-cybernised young man that his mother was a robot. 'I know,' he said instead. 'I'm sorry, but we have to be patient. Wait for our moment.'

'To do what? You said the power would flow

back into their systems and overload them.'

'You seem to have picked up some of the Cybermen's technical understanding, from being connected to their network. But I had to disconnect you to keep you human. I thought I'd reconnected you just to the energy pathways, but obviously it didn't work.'

'So the power can't get through.'

'Not unless we plug you into their systems some other way. Find a route that's unprotected. These Cybermen will have safety cut-outs, firewalls, the lot.'

At the base of the tower, Marie Ernhardt lay sprawled across the stone-flagged courtyard. Her body was crumpled, one side of her head smashed in. Her long fair hair spread out round her head, framing the shattered remains of her pale, delicate features. Cogs and gears lay strewn where they had fallen. Oil was leaking from her eyes, like dark tears.

The Doctor and Victor stopped to look down at her, to spare her a few moments' thought. If Victor was surprised at what he saw, he did not show it. But the Cybermen herded them on again, towards a door into the main castle.

'Where are you taking us?' Victor asked. But he got no reply.

A trickle of dust fell from the tunnel roof. The door shook. It was braced with metal, but the main construction was wood, and that was splintering under repeated blows from the other side.

Jedka sat huddled and trembling between her mother and Olga. Other children and their parents lined the tunnel. Ahead of them, the way was blocked. Behind, the door shook and splintered. No one spoke. No one pretended that everything would be all right.

At the far end of the tunnel, Nicolai and Klaus were talking in low voices with Lord Ernhardt as they examined the bricked-up end wall that prevented them getting any further. But it was obvious to everyone that the Plague Warriors would be in long before the wall could be dismantled.

'My daddy will save us,' Jedka said.

A metal fist punched through the door.

'Why have you brought us here?' the Doctor asked, looking round the Watchman's work room. 'Not that I'm ungrateful,' he added, giving Victor a meaningful look. 'Lots of useful stuff in here. Ah!' he realised. 'Is that it?'

'You will repair the power converter,' one of the Cybermen intoned. 'Or you will build a new one.'

'Using equipment the Watchman salvaged.'

The Doctor walked slowly round the Watchman's workbench. He picked up a few components, then discarded them again. 'Why me?'

'You have superior intelligence to the other humans.'

He didn't deny it. 'Why not do it yourselves? Is it because I understand the way the Watchman worked, and how he's tried to adapt some of this stuff? Or maybe you just like getting others to do your work, is that it?'

The Cybermen did not answer. The Doctor had made a complete tour of the table now, and was back with Victor. The Doctor hoped the Cybermen wouldn't realise he was talking to him and not them.

'All along you were giving the Watchman instructions, weren't you? Relayed through what he thought was a miraculous Oracle that guided his work. But you were using him, getting him to develop and repair the components that you needed. Scavenging the parts to make a new power converter.'

The Doctor was walking again as he spoke. Now he was close to the curtained alcove. He grabbed the curtain and pulled it back, revealing he plinth covered by a sheet.

'What is it?' Victor asked.

'The Watchman's Oracle. Damaged, but still connected into the Cyber networks, still part of your systems so that you could hear if not see what the Watchman was up to. So you could relay instructions. It might not have achieved much but, oh, you are a patient lot, aren't you. Every little bit helps.'

The nearest Cyberman took a step towards the Doctor. 'You will build a power converter. We will re-energise. We will survive.'

The Doctor shook his head. 'No, I don't think so, thanks all the same.'

The Cyberman took another step forwards. The Doctor took hold of the sheet and pulled it off the plinth – revealing the damaged Cyber-head beneath, with its empty eye sockets.

At once, the head screamed – just as it had before. The Cyberman grabbed the Doctor, dragging him back. The other Cybermen crowded round him.

'Victor!' the Doctor yelled above the electronic howls of pain and anguish. 'Victor – you know what to do. You can save them. You can save everyone. The link's still open. The power will flow through you.'

Two of the Cybermen turned quickly towards Victor, perhaps realising the danger. But they were too late.

Victor stepped forward, reached out, and grabbed the Cyber-head on the plinth between both his metal hands.

Its screaming reached an ear-shattering peak. The head exploded.

Moments later, the same power that had overloaded the head flowed through into the main Cyber systems and on to each of the Cybermen.

The Doctor threw himself to the floor as the Cybermen round him detonated. Metal and plastic blasted across the room. The Cybermen advancing on Victor also exploded. One toppled forwards, bursting into flames before it hit the ground.

The first of the Plague Warriors forced its way through the shattered remains of the door and into the tunnel. The villagers backed away, as far down the passage as they could get. Olga felt Jedka clutch at her skirts. Somehow Klaus was beside her, his arm round her shoulders.

'There are things I meant to tell you,' he said quietly. 'I guess it's too late now. I'm sorry.'

Despite everything, Olga smiled. 'I'm sorry, too,' she said.

But her words were lost in the rumble of thunder from outside – a rolling wall of noise that grew closer and closer. Flames erupted through the doorway behind the Plague Warrior. A moment later, the metal creature itself was on fire, its arms lashing out, a harsh electronic screech echoing round the tunnel walls. It fell forwards into a pool of fire.

The Doctor ran to Victor. The young man sank to his metal knees. His face was grey and drawn.

'It's drained the power from you,' the Doctor said. He caught the man – barely more than a boy, as he fell sideways. Cradled him in his arms.

'I have been wasting away all my life, Doctor.' His voice was barely audible. 'At least this way I helped. I *did* something.'

The Doctor was still holding him minutes later when the door burst open. A hand reached under the Doctor's, supporting Victor's head. Lord Ernhardt took his place and held his dying son in his arms one last time.

The villagers were gathered in the courtyard. A pall of smoke hung in the air high above, defying the rain that tried to wash it away.

Olga and Klaus sat together by a wall, their arms round each other.

A little way away, Nicolai was tending to Gustav the tavern keeper. His wounds were serious, but not fatal.

All around lay the shattered, broken remains of the Plague Warriors – the Cybermen.

A little girl stood beside one smoking metal body, staring out through the broken remains of the main gates. Her mother stood beside her as they both stared out across the valley.

The Doctor walked through it all, head down, mentally counting the cost. He looked up only when Jedka called to him.

'Are you her mother?' he asked. 'She's a good girl. She's been a terrific help. You should be proud of her.'

'I am,' the mother said, but her words were almost a sob.

'When's my daddy coming back?' Jedka asked.

She wasn't crying, but her eyes were brimming ready. 'He looks after us. He keeps us safe.'

'I don't know,' the Doctor said. He knelt down so he could talk to her eye to eye. 'I'm afraid I don't know who your daddy is, Jedka.'

'He's a guard. He works here at the castle. Why isn't he here?'

'A guard with a daughter he'd die for,' the Doctor said quietly. 'Your father was a very brave man. He fought hard so that someone else very brave, a young man called Victor, could save us all.'

'Then where is he?'

'Oh, Jedka,' her mother said through her tears, and pulled her into a hug.

'Will he be coming home soon?' Jedka asked, but she was crying now too.

The Doctor opened his mouth to say something, though he had no idea what.

Then the answer came from behind him:

'Of course I am. I'll be home as soon as I've got this mess cleared up.'

The Doctor spun round. Caplan was covered in grime and blood. There was a cut down one side of his face, and his left arm hung limply by his side. But he was smiling as his daughter ran to him. He hugged her with his good arm, nodded at the Doctor, then leaned forward to rest his head on his wife's quaking shoulder.

The Doctor watched them for a moment, their

bodies trembling with emotion. Then he turned and walked away.

The Doctor spent all day and all night in the Watchman's lair. He emerged the next day, looking exhausted but smiling, to find Lord Ernhardt sitting by the fire, where they had first met.

The room was a mess. The door was off its hinges, there were scorch marks on the floor and ceiling. The remains of broken chairs and a table were heaped in a corner.

'You've finished?' Lord Ernhardt asked. He got unsteadily to his feet. He seemed to have aged, and of course he was now missing one hand.

'The Cybership powered down when the Cybermen exploded,' the Doctor said. 'It'll rot down there, eventually. But seal up the tunnels and let no one near it. The radiation will fade in time, but it'll take a while. And I've destroyed or made safe everything the Watchman had salvaged.

'Thank you, Doctor.'

'No – thank *you*. You've given far more than I ever could. Paid a price that can never be repaid.'

'Nevertheless, Doctor – thank you.'

They shook hands.

'You will be leaving now, I suppose. Going back to wherever you are from?'

'I'm from everywhere and nowhere. But yes, I'm leaving.' He hesitated in the doorway. 'I can never give you back your son, but you will always have his memory.'

'He would have died years ago if it weren't for the Watchman, and for the Cybermen. They gave him life, albeit unwittingly and unwillingly. They gave me that memory. So it's fitting that it was Victor who saved us from them.'

The Doctor nodded. 'Like I said, I can never return him to you. But the Watchman was a clever old thing. I wish I'd had time to get to know him better. He gave you far more than I ever could, though I have done what I can. He gave you hope for the future.'

Lord Ernhardt forced a thin smile. 'A lonely future now, I fear.'

'Oh I wouldn't say that. You should get involved in village life more,' the Doctor said. 'Both of you.'

'Both?'

But the Doctor was gone.

Another figure stood in the doorway where he had just been. A young woman with long fair hair and pale, delicate features.

Lord Ernhardt caught his breath, felt his heart leap in his chest. 'Marie?'

Olga and Klaus walked with him out of the village. The Doctor had joined them for a drink at the tavern with Old Nicolai and the others. Jedka ran out of her house to wave as the Doctor walked with Olga and Klaus along the dirt track past the church and the graveyard. For once, it wasn't raining. Now the equipment in the church tower was gone, the Doctor had promised the weather in the valley would improve.

'Where are you going?' Olga asked.

'Not far,' the Doctor said. 'Or there again, further than you can ever imagine.'

As they climbed the winding, steep pathway, they paused to turn and look back across the valley at the castle.

'I can't help noticing,' the Doctor said, 'that you two are holding hands.'

'We've often held hands,' Klaus told him, slightly sheepish.

'Though not since we were at school,' Olga added. 'And they say you're only young once,' she added with a smile.

'Well, they're wrong,' the Doctor said. 'I've been young lots of times. I can recommend it. Just wait here a minute, will you?'

He didn't give them time to answer, but hurried round a bend in the track and disappeared. Klaus and Olga looked at each other. They waited a moment, but the Doctor didn't return.

'You think he's just leaving?' Klaus asked.

'Perhaps he doesn't like saying goodbye,' Olga said.

Their conversation was interrupted by a strange

scraping, grinding noise. They ran after the Doctor. But by the time they had turned the corner, the sound was gone. The path straightened out and from here they could see for miles. The path, the open, barren countryside... There was nowhere for anyone to hide, nothing to obscure the view.

But of the Doctor there was no sign.

'Well look at that,' Olga said in astonishment as the empty landscape was bathed in a pale yellow glow. 'The sun's come out.'

Hand in hand, Olga and Klaus walked slowly back to the village.

Somewhere infinitely far away, but separated from them by only a few seconds, a lonely figure stood at the heart of his TARDIS. A slim mismatched jigsaw of a man, paintbrush hair atop a young face with ancient eyes, an enigma wrapped in a bow tie.

'I'm getting far too young for this sort of thing,' he said to himself. The TARDIS groaned, as if in reply. Lights blinked and needles wavered on dials. Gauges and read-outs told their stories and the glass column at the heart of the TARDIS console rose and fell and glowed and shone.

And the Doctor stared off into space and time, wondering where his oldest and best friend would take him next.

BBC

DOCTOR WHO

The Dalek Generation

NICHOLAS BRIGGS

'*The Sunlight Worlds offer you a life of comfort and plenty. Apply for your brand new home now, by contacting us at the Dalek Foundation.*'

Sunlight 349 is one of countless Dalek Foundation worlds, planets created to house billions of humanoids suffering from economic hardship. The Doctor arrives at Sunlight 349, suspicious of any world where the Daleks are apparently a force for good – and determined to find out the truth.

He soon finds himself in court, facing the 'Dalek Litigator'. But do his arch enemies really have nothing more to threaten than legal action? The Doctor knows they have a far more sinister plan – but how can he convince those who have lived under the benevolence of the Daleks for a generation?

Convince them he must, and soon. For on another Foundation planet, archaeologists have unearthed the most dangerous technology in the universe…

A thrilling, all-new adventure featuring the Doctor as played by Matt Smith in the spectacular hit series from BBC Television.

U.S. $9.99 (Canada: $11.99) ISBN: 978-0-385-34674-0

BBC

DOCTOR WHO

Shroud of Sorrow

TOMMY DONBAVAND

23 November 1963

It is the day after John F. Kennedy's assassination
– and the faces of the dead are everywhere. PC Reg
Cranfield sees his recently deceased father in the mists
along Totter's Lane. Reporter Mae Callon sees her late
grandmother in a coffee stain on her desk. FBI Special
Agent Warren Skeet finds his long-dead partner staring
back at him from raindrops on a window pane.

Then the faces begin to talk, and scream… and push
through into our world.

As the alien Shroud begins to feast on the grief of a
world in mourning, can the Doctor dig deep enough into
his own sorrow to save mankind?

*A thrilling, all-new adventure featuring the Doctor and Clara,
as played by Matt Smith and Jenna-Louise Coleman in the
spectacular hit series from BBC Television.*

U.S. $9.99 (Canada: $11.99) ISBN: 978-0-385-34678-8